Sunlight City, A Mystical Knight Novel
By Jade Stephenson ©.

CW01465879

Copyright © 2022 Jade Stephenson

All rights reserved.

The characters and events portrayed in this book are fictitious. Any similarity to real persons, living or dead, is coincidental and not intended by the author. No part of this book may be reproduced, or stored in a retrieval system, or transmitted in any form or by any means, electronic, mechanical, photocopying, recording, or otherwise, without express written permission of the publisher.

Cover design, map and crest by: Jade Stephenson using Clip Studio Paint.

Sunlight City, A Mystical Knight Novel book 2.
By Jade Stephenson ©.

Contents

Sunlight City, A Mystical Knight Novel book 2.
By Jade Stephenson ©.

Sunlight City, A Mystical Knight Novel book 2.
By Jade Stephenson ©.

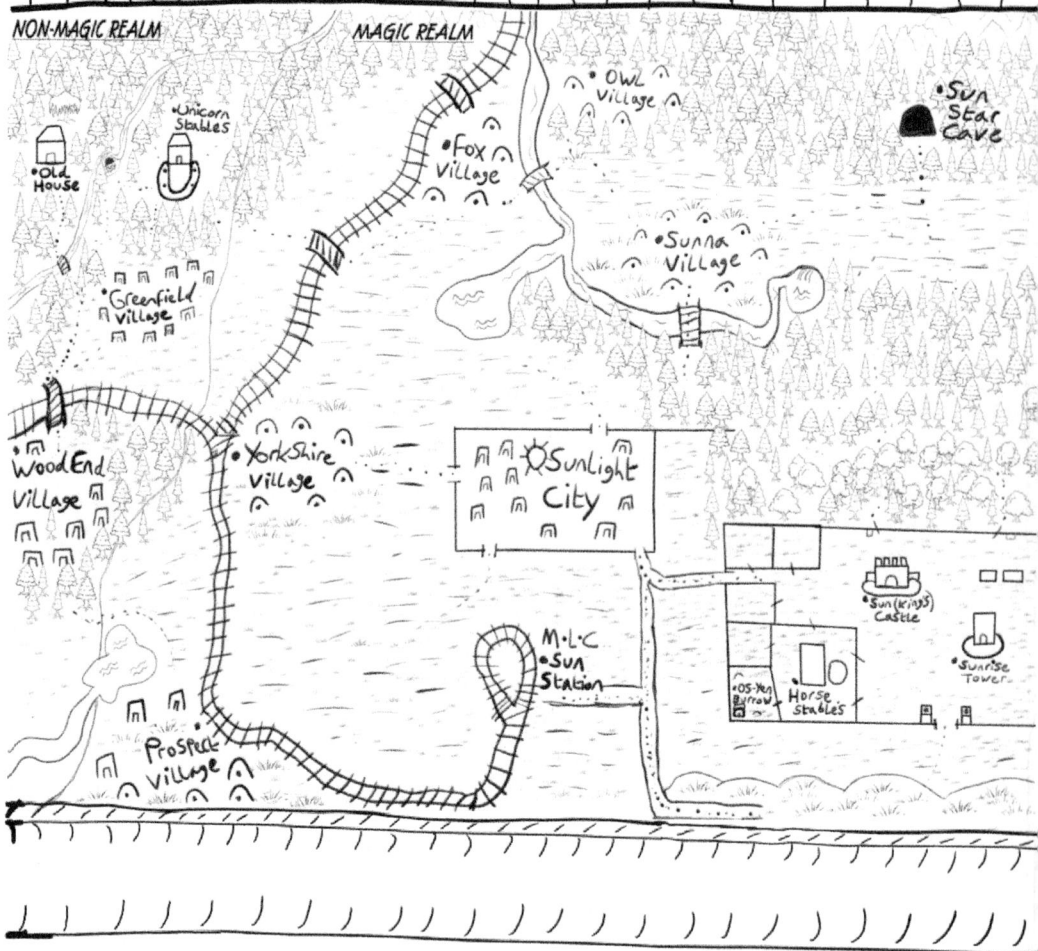

Sunlight City.
A Mystical Knight Novel, Book 2.

Prologue.

In a land far, far away, lies the kingdom of Roseberry and in the center of that kingdom sits Sunlight City, a large peaceful city full of wonder and magic.

Here is where the Shapeshifter King lives with his guards and knights, the knights help protect the king and other magic users from magical threats and they also collect magical items. These knights are known as the Mystical Knights.

Chapter 1.
On the way to Sunlight City.

"Good boy, don't worry we will be there soon. I hope." I said to my black horse Silver.

As I patted him on the neck, he looked at me with worry in his big silver eyes that gleamed in the sunlight that was shining through the cracks of the large stable carriage.
We were both riding in an M.L.C. Which is a magical land carrier that can transport people, animals, and items to faraway lands that are too far to travel by horse or if you want to get somewhere quicker, this is the best way. The M.L.C. glides along tracks on the ground and is powered by coal, sunlight, and magic.

"Next stop Sunlight City, please take your seats for the next part of our journey." Said a man's voice through the echo stone on the wall.

I sighed out loud and gave Silver one last pat before heading off through the M.L.C. to get to the dining cart where the best windows were, so I could see the views outside.
As the stable carriage was the last one on the M.L.C. I had to walk through two storage carts that were filled with everyone's luggage and goods, then three-room carts where people would stay overnight if needed, then I walked through the next door to the dining cart. I sat down in an empty seat closest to the door so I could leave quickly once we got to the next station.
The journey had been a long one, first I had to

leave Greenfield Village and ride to Wood End Village so I could get on to the M.L.C. at the station there. My friend Nick had come with me on his horse Murphy to see me off and make sure I got on board alright. It had been hard for me to say goodbye to my family and friends, but I knew it was time for me to leave.

I have the jewel of darkness, a magical item I wear around my neck like a necklace, it is a pointed hexagon shaped jewel that is purple but when you look closer you can see many colors, it also changes colors when I use the magic stored within.
By law anyone with a strong magical item connected to them must live in Sunlight City so the Mystical Knights can help protect them and make sure they are not using the magic within for anything bad.

Though instead of just moving to the city I have decided to train and become a Mystical Knight myself so I can help my friends protect the land and its people with my magic. I was supposed to move to Sunlight City earlier to start my training straight away but I wasn't ready, so Robert Odin a Mystical Knight everyone just calls Odin and who is like a father to me as I never knew my real one, got special permission from the shapeshifter king Eric Hart, to let me stay longer as I wasn't yet ready to leave and I wanted to help Unicorn Stables more before I left.
We had spent our time working hard building new horse stables at a nearby village and then a bad snow storm hit over the winter months, so I was told by Odin it would be safer to stay put than to

travel by horse as the M.L.C. was not allowed to be used during the bad weather.

Then springtime arrived with me celebrating my sixteenth birthday and then Anthony and Helen got married, so of course I had to stay for that, I was a bridesmaid after all. Nicks parents also had a new baby girl, and they named her Lilly, after my mother.

It was a great time to spend the last moments with my family and friends at Greenfield Village, the time flew by and before I realized it ten months had past. It was now time for me to start my new life at Sunlight City, I could have stayed longer but I was ready now.

I smiled and looked down at my bracelet; before I left, Nick had given me a new silver horse charm for it, I had placed it next to my wooden black panther charm that my friend Tristan had given me before. The bracelet was my mothers, and it also held a tiger, a heart, and a fairy charm too, I hope it will bring me luck at my new home.

I looked back up and watched the world roll by outside, I had seen a lot of interesting sights on this journey, but me and Silver just wanted to get off this M.L.C. now. We had been riding it for half a day, luckily, we could get off at every stop to stretch our legs, but it had been harder for me to persuade Silver to get back on.

I was also getting excited knowing I would see my friends again soon, while they had stayed at Greenfield Village we had become close, they were like a second family, so I had missed them a lot when they had to return to Sunlight City. I had kept in touch with them using the S.C.D. the

device that lets you talk to people far away without
using letters, but it only works for people who have
magical energy inside them, so I still wrote some
letters to them too.

Odin had told me the two fairy sisters, Marigold
and Clover would be meeting me at the station so
they could both ride back with me to Sun Castle.

Sun Castle was the home of the shapeshifter king
and in the grounds of the castle was a building
called Sunrise Tower where some of the Mystical
knights live, it would also become my new home.

There was a loud screech as the M.L.C. came to a
halt; we had finally arrived at the station. I jumped
up out of my seat and was first out of the door, I
then headed to the back of the M.L.C. to get Silver
off too. I had tacked him up earlier and left the one
bag that I carried with him attached to his saddle
so it would be quicker to leave. Luckily, my other
bags and boxes had been delivered to Sunlight
City earlier in the year so they would be all ready
in my room when I arrived.

I spotted Silver with Max the stable boy at the end
of the platform.

"Here you are Miss Rose, I hope you and Silver
enjoy living at Sunlight City." He said and handed
me Silvers reins.

Silver nuzzled his curly black hair which made
Max laugh, I smiled, Max had helped us a lot on
this journey even though he was only ten he was a
strong boy who we would both miss.

"Thank you for everything Max, you can come
visit us any time you like."

"Alright I will, goodbye Miss Rose and Silver." He said, then he left to go help another man with his horse.

"Come on then Silver lets go find Marigold and Clover." I said and looked around.

The platform was busy with people getting off the M.L.C. and others who were waiting to get on for the next journey. I couldn't see the sisters so I headed down the track away from the platform leading Silver, I felt him pull on his reins and knew he could sense them nearby and he was right, we rounded the next corner, and they were there waiting for us sat on top of their horses Blue and Betty.

"Hello Rose." Shouted Clover, and Marigold waved.

"Hello, we are finally here." I said and stopped in front of them.

Marigold laughed "I'm glad, we missed you Rose."

"I missed you too and it looks like Silver missed your girls." I laughed as Silver nuzzled Blue and Betty in greeting.

I had stayed in contact with Marigold and Clover the most, so I was happy to see them again.

"So, are you ready to see your new home?" Asked Marigold.

"Yes, let's go." I said and climbed onto Silvers back.

We set off down the stone path at a steady walk and I could tell Silver was happy to be off the

M.L.C. He was having a good look around as we walked and seemed excited about the new location.

I pulled my hood up as the rain started to fall, it was the middle of summer here but today it felt cooler, the clouds had gathered, and the wind had picked up. We suddenly came to a fork in the road and stopped our horses.

"If you go that way it will take you to the city." Explained Marigold as she pointed left.

I looked down the road and in the distance I could see the grey roofs of many old buildings.

"And this way is the way to your new home." Said Clover and she walked Betty to the right, down the other road and we followed her.

"The castle isn't too far from the city but it's far enough away to give us all more space and it's quieter too. You can also walk into the city from the other side of the castle, so once you settle in, you can go to the shops and explore whenever you like. This way takes us over the large meadow field in front of the castle so our horses can have a good run when needed." Marigold explained as we followed Clover down the road.

I nodded and took in my surroundings, the landscape was beautiful, and it reminded me of home at Greenfield Village as it also had many open fields, but Sunlight City had more moorlands.

We got to the top of the hill and from there we could finally see the top of the king's large castle

and the large stone tower next to it must be the Mystical Knights home and the place I would live from now on. The grounds and both buildings were both surrounded by a large wall that had two smaller towers at the large gate.
I smiled and was about to comment on the look of my new home when I suddenly sensed something behind me, the horses knew something was wrong too, and Silver side-stepped to the right quickly so I had to grab hold of his mane so I wouldn't fall off. I looked behind me and noticed what the problem was.

"Oh No." Shouted Clover.

There were at least a dozen shadow demons in wolf form ready to chase us.

"Run." Shouted Marigold.

Chapter 2.
New Home.

Blue and Betty took off at a fast canter down the hill towards the open field, before Silver followed them, I quickly sent off a wave of magic from the jewel of darkness which took out the nearest shadow demons before they started to chase us.

I heard the dreaded sound of drumming which usually meant more shadow demons were coming, Silver quickly caught up with Blue and Betty as more shadow demons appeared from behind some bushes as though they were waiting for us. As we got into the open field, bells started to ring out from the castle grounds, before I could figure out what that meant I heard a scream beside me and noticed Marigold had fell off Blue.

"Sister!" Shouted Clover.
  "Clover go!" I yelled and pointed towards the castle.

She nodded in understanding and told Betty to go faster as she followed Blue to the gates.
I quickly turned Silver back around and we headed towards Marigold who was picking herself up off the ground.

"I can't fly; I can't change. I think I've broke my arm." She said as she tried to catch her breath.

When fairies get hurt too badly, they can't change into their smaller fairy form until they are fully healed. I knew I could fix her arm with my magic, but I knew right now I needed to get us both to the castle and there was another form of magic I needed to use that used up a lot of my energy, I jumped off Silver.

"Get on Silver." I yelled and helped her climb on, then I took out a nearby demon with my dagger I got out of my belt.

The other shadows came closer, so I fired off more magic then shouted, "Silver go!"
  "Wait, what about you?" Yelled Marigold.

"I will be fine, now go."
I saw Silver hesitate, so I gave him a hard pat on his flank, he huffed then took off at a steady canter to help Marigold stay on. I glanced at the gate and could see other Mystical Knights and a few Kings Guards getting ready to fight and I also saw a black panther running towards me.
I smiled and turned back around as more shadow demons got closer, this time they were in the form of men with large swords, I wasn't worried though as I knew what magic to use.

I knelt down and slammed my hand to the wet ground; I connected to the earth's power and the jewel of darkness lit up a bright green as I cast the spell of protection. My magic built up a large green glass dome that surrounded me and the castle to protect everyone inside. I spread the magic shield far and wide before I disconnected from my magic. I then sat down on the grass as the dizzy spells started, the spell had took up a lot of my energy but at least I didn't pass out like I had the first time I had used it.

I watched the shadow demons crash against the
dome, they hissed and screamed frustrated they
could not get through, then one by one they
started to disappear.
I heard voices behind me, the knights and guards
had come. I slowly tried to stand but I was still
weak and feeling dizzy, so I fell back down, then I
heard a voice in my head.

"**Rose?**" Said Tristan the shapeshifter.
   I looked up and hugged the large black panther
beside me.
   "**Hello Tristan.**" I replied through our mind link then
laughed out loud.

It had been a while since we had spoken like this,
we share a rare gift called mental link, it's a magic
that helps you communicate with each other
through your minds by thinking. You can
sometimes also feel what the other is feeling and
share dreams. I could only do it with Tristan and I
still wasn't sure why we had that connection.

I suddenly heard people drawing their swords from
their sheaths, I glanced up and noticed men in red
uniforms pointing their swords at me, they were
the Kings Guards. I let go of Tristan and slowly put
my hands up. Tristan growled at the men but
before I could say anything I heard a familiar voice
shout.
   "Stand down!"

The guards lowered their weapons and Odin
walked up to us.
"Rose are you alright?" He asked.

"Yes I'm fine, just tired. That was some welcome home party." I smiled and tried to stand up again, this time I stayed on my feet.

Silver walked back over to me without Marigold riding him, she must have got off at the gate so Silver could come back for me. I gave him a pat on the neck.
  "You were great Silver." I said.

He neighed, then bent his head down to nuzzle Tristan. I smiled, even though Tristan was in his panther form Silver wasn't scared of him.

"So Rose, I see you can use your magic again." Said Odin as he looked around at the magic shield I had put up, he did not look happy.

I had completely forgotten I was supposed to keep that fact a secret, until they remove the magic repel band on my arm, that they had put on me at Greenfield Village before they left, as the king did not want me using my magic while I stayed there, sadly though I had to remove it myself due to problems it was causing me, but I had not told them as I didn't want them to get into any trouble.
  "Um, yeah. Sorry." I replied.

Odin sighed and said, "Come on lets go to my office, I think you need to explain some things to me."

He walked off in the direction of the castle and the other Mystical Knights and King's Guards followed him, but I noticed them glancing at me with worried looks as though they were scared of me. I glanced down at the jewel; it had faded back down to purple again. I felt fur brush up against my hand, it was Tristan. He blinked his large green eyes at me then walked off to catch up with the others, I took hold of Silver's reins and followed him to the large gate in front of us.

As we entered the gate, I looked up in wonder at the two large towers beside it, and on top of the towers were the bells I had heard ringing earlier, I guess they must have rang them as a warning the shadow demons were coming.

"Thank you Rose." Said Marigold as she came to stand beside me with Clover.
 "It's alright, are you OK?" I asked.
She smiled sadly and nodded.

"Marigold go to the medical room, and Clover could you take Silver to the stables and get him settled in; I need to discuss some things with Rose." Said Odin in a stern voice.

Marigold left and Clover took Silver's reins from me.
 "Silver be good for Clover." I said as I took my bag from the saddle then I whispered to Clover, "It sounds like I might be in trouble."

Clover laughed then walked off with Silver in the direction of the stables, I would have to remember that later as the castle grounds looked massive, I would definitely be getting lost a lot in this new place.
I headed right with Odin to the Mystical Knights home or H.Q. as Edmund likes to call it. Before I

followed Odin up the marble steps to the door I stopped and looked up, I couldn't believe this was now my new home. There were many windows on the stone tower and on the top floor it looked like a sheet of glass went all the way around and it had a triangle shaped roof. A sign was at the bottom of the steps, and it read 'Sunrise Tower.'

"Come along Rose, you can explore later."
Shouted Odin, who was already holding the door open for me.

I quickly ran up the steps and Odin finally smiled at me as he noticed the amazed look on my face. I walked through the door and all the different colors, scents, and sounds hit me at once, it was a large open entrance hall where many different people wearing red King's Guards and blue Mystical Knights uniforms were busy walking about and talking to each other. Also, the middle of the tower looked like a garden.

"Is that a garden inside?" I asked and looked down at Tristan who was stood beside me.
   "Yes, wait until you see the rest of the place, you're going to love it." He replied through my mind.

"Up here." Odin shouted as he headed up some stairs on my right, I guess I will have to look closer at the garden later; I thought, and I hurried after him up the stairs.

"Rose!" I heard a familiar voice shout as we reached the second floor.
   Isabella pulled me into a hug, "Welcome to your new home."

"Hello Isabella, thank you." I replied.

"I heard what happened and I saw your magic shield; it covered the entire castle grounds. How did you do that?" She asked.

"Um."

"She can tell us in here." Said Odin and he held open another door.

I shrugged my shoulders and followed him into the room, Isabella, and Tristan still in his panther form followed us. I smiled as I entered the room, it reminded me of the room in Old House at Greenfield Village, this also must be Odin's office. I looked around the room that was filled with many books, old looking objects, and weapons. Odin walked over to the desk unbuckled his sword from his belt and sat down in the large chair. He pointed to the seat opposite him and looked at me. I smiled, put my bag down, took off my wet cloak and sat down, Isabella sat next to Odin, and Tristan climbed up onto the window seat behind them and laid down, but he kept his eyes on us as he licked his paws dry.

"So Rose, can you please explain how you can use magic again?" Asked Odin.

Chapter 3.
New Room.

I took a deep breath and pulled the magic repel band out of my bag and laid it down onto the desk in front of us.
The Mystical Knights had given it to me at Greenfield Village, I was supposed to wear it while living there to stop me using my magic, as the king had instructed, he did not want me using my magic without a Mystical Knight present. I was going to put it back on my arm again before they noticed I had taken it off, but I guess it was too late for that.

"I wore it for a few weeks after you left but then I started to become unwell, and it hurt my arm." I explained and rolled up my sleeve to show them the burn mark, it was still there even though I heal faster than most, and I still didn't know why.

"Rose...." Said Odin as he looked at my arm in shock.
"Don't worry I'm alright now." I said.
I didn't want him to blame himself as he had been the one to put the band on me.

"How did you remove it though? Only a Mystical Knight would know the code." Asked Isabella.
"Well luckily Lucas figured it out for me." I smiled as I remembered my old friend.

He was Tristan's older brother, and he carried the jewel of darkness before me, but an accident happened, and he lost control of the magic inside

and died, though a part of his soul somehow
attached itself onto the jewel so I started to see his
spirit in reflections and in my dreams so he helped
me whenever he could.
Sadly though, a few months ago I stopped seeing
him, when I had called Odin and Tristan on the
S.C.D. to tell them, Odin had explained he may
have moved on as I no longer needed him.

"That still doesn't explain why you kept this from
us." Said Odin in a mad voice.
   "I'm sorry, I didn't want you to get into trouble
from the king and I knew you would want me to
move here sooner to make sure I wasn't using my
magic, but I couldn't. I wasn't ready to leave my
home yet." I replied.

Odin sighed "I would have just sent out a Mystical
Knight to keep an eye on you, I probably would
have gone myself, you should never have hidden
that from us. Anything could have happened to
you."

I nodded and decided not to tell them how bad I
got; I had nearly died wearing the band. Lucas
believed it was sucking up too much of my magic
from the jewel, so to recover, the jewel was taking
my energy in return which caused me to become
weak and unwell, luckily I could still see Lucas in
my dreams, and he told me the word to remove
the band.
If he hadn't been there who knows what would
have happened to me. I had made my family at
Unicorn Stables promise me they would not tell
the Mystical Knights, maybe I will one day but not
now.

"Rose what else are you hiding from us?" asked Tristan through our mind link. He must have sensed my feelings of sadness and worry.

I smiled at him and said out loud "I am sorry, but I have been using my magic again too."

Odin slammed his hand down on the desk, it made me jump.
"That was foolish, the Dark Shadow Guild could have easily sensed your presence there and tried to take the jewel or even you with them. That was one of the reasons why we put the magic repel band on you, so they would believe you had travelled here with us. Also, you could have easily lost control of your magic and caused some serious damage or even hurt someone again."

"I know but sometimes my magic would work by accident, so I thought learning how to use it would keep it under control, also Lucas believed I would become stronger and learn how to live with the jewel. I didn't want to lose control again and I knew teaching myself control would help. I promised Lucas and my family I would contact you straight away if I sensed I was in trouble or if the Dark Shadow Guild would return. I haven't seen any shadow demons since that day in the forest, well until now anyway. I don't know why they were chasing us." I explained.

"We understand Rose but that was still reckless, you definitely should have told one of us." Said Isabella.
"Sorry." I said.

Odin sighed and got up from his chair, he grabbed his sword and walked over to the door. "We all need to trust each other here; you need to remember that, if you want to become a Mystical Knight. We will talk more later; I need to go and explain to the Mystic Council why there is now a magical barrier up around the castle. I suggest you get some sleep; you look like you need it, and Tristan go back to the castle the guards will be wondering where you have gone." With that said he left the office.

I looked at Isabella and Tristan and said, "I guess he is going to be mad for a while."

"You know how he gets; he is only worried about you. And seeing your eyes like that again probably shocked him." Explained Isabella.
  "My eyes?" I asked.
"They have gone red again, well only one has this time." Said Isabella.

I blinked and pulled out my small mirror I always carried from the pouch on my belt. I looked at my reflection, she was right, one eye had turned red while the other had stayed brown. That must have been why the guards were staring at me. It had happened once before when I had accidentally used too much magic, I had lost control and killed Caleb, I had passed out afterwards and was asleep for three days, so I understood why they were worried.

"Don't worry, I'm alright but I am tired it was a long journey here." I said and put my mirror away.

"Well, I'm glad you are here now, we did miss you. Come on I will show you to your new room." Said Isabella and she stood up and walked over to the door.

"I missed everyone too." I said and followed her.

Tristan followed us out of the door, but he turned to walk off in the opposite direction.

"**I will see you later, I hope you like your new home.**" He said through my mind, then he ran back down the stairs we had come up.

"I think you will like your new room; the prince chose it for you." Smiled Isabella.

Prince? And then I remembered, Tristan was now the prince of Sunlight City. When the king becomes a certain age and has not had children of his own, he can choose a suitable person to rule after him. As the shapeshifter king has no children and as he helped raise Tristan and Lucas, he chose Lucas to be next in line for the throne but now Tristan has that responsibility.
They had not told me when they had lived at Greenfield Village, but Marigold had said the king wasn't sure if Tristan had wanted to carry on after Lucas had died so it wasn't certain until later. I was shocked to learn I was friends with a prince and that must also be why the guards had acted the way they had when I had hugged Tristan, that was probably not the right way to greet him.

"Oh right, I forgot. Maybe I should have bowed." I smiled, as we headed to another set of stairs in front of us.

"No, it's alright, you are one of his best friends so he would hate it if you acted differently towards him now." Said Isabella as we started climbing up the spiral staircase that was in the middle of the tower.

I looked down and I could see the pretty little indoor garden, it had a fountain in the middle, people were sat around it reading books.
As we climbed up the stairs I looked up and noticed how big the tower was, it was huge, and right on the top of the roof I could see a large stained-glass window that was letting the sun shine through. The window had a picture of many animals, it was beautiful. We climbed up a lot of stairs and I was definitely feeling tired now, then Isabella held open a door for me.
As we entered Isabella said, "This is the fifth floor where our rooms are, there are thirteen bedrooms on this floor and twelve on the floor beneath us. Don't worry you will get used to the stairs." She laughed as she saw the tired look on my face.
We walked around the corridor, and I noticed all the rooms had numbers on the doors, we stopped at number twenty-three.
"This is your room, number twenty-four is Tristan's and number twenty-two is Edmunds room, my room is number twenty-six between Odin's and Marigold's rooms." Said Isabella, then she opened the door and walked in.

I smiled and followed her inside; I was happy I would be near the Mystical Knights I thought of as my second family.
Once in the room I dropped my bag onto the floor and looked around, the first thing I noticed was the

shape of the room, it was curved to fit inside the tower. All my boxes had been stacked up near a small desk, there were large cupboards on one wall and the bed was at the back of the room next to the large window.
I also noticed another door, Isabella saw me looking so she opened it and explained, "This is your toilet and sink, every bedroom has one but if you want a bath or shower you will have to go back down to the second floor."

Wow, this room is a lot bigger than the one I had at Unicorn Stables, I thought.
I then noticed the wall near the cupboards opposite the bed, it was full of photographs and a shelf held wooden animal figures, that I noticed were mainly horses and big cats. I walked over to the wall to have a look at the photos and realized a lot of them were of Lucas with other people or animals.

"This room used to belong to Lucas, he loved taking photographs with his stone lens and posing in them too. He always said he wanted to remember his memories and have some way to always look back at them whenever he wanted, so he normally took a stone lens out with him wherever he went."

"Are you sure it's alright for me to have this room?" I asked.
   "Of course it is, I think you are the only one who can have it. Tristan didn't want anyone in this room before, but when he heard Odin was trying to decide what room to give you, he said you could have this one, he also said you would like the view

outside the window." Isabella smiled and pointed at the window.

I walked over to the window and noticed it was also a door; I pushed it open and stepped out onto a small balcony. It was still raining and cloudy, but you could see for miles, and when I looked to my right, I could see the castle but what made me smile the most, was the views of the horse stables and fields in front as it reminded me of home. Tristan was right, I loved the view outside my window.

"So, what do you think, will this be alright for you?" Asked Isabella behind me.

"It's fantastic, thank you." I smiled.

I walked back inside and looked again at the photos. Lucas had a lot of friends, I bet they miss him a lot. I know I do, and I wish I could still see him.

"If you want to take the photos down, you can. It's your room now." Said Isabella as she noticed the sad look on my face.

"No, I will keep them up, we have to remember Lucas's memories."

"Alright, well I will leave you to rest. Dinner will be served in the cafeteria soon; a bell will ring to let you know once it's ready. The cafeteria is on the first floor, your diary and maps of the tower and grounds are on your desk so you shouldn't get lost, but if you do just ask anyone and they will help you."

"Alright, thank you Isabella."

"Your welcome, see you later." Said Isabella as she waved and left the room.

Once the door was shut, I sighed out loud then collapsed onto my new bed, I was exhausted, using that much magic plus the long journey here and walking up all those stairs finally caught up with me, my eyes drifted shut and I fell asleep.

Chapter 4.
Ghosts.

After another nightmare of shadows chasing me, I woke up to the sound of a loud bell, once I remembered where I was, I realized the sound of the bell was a different sound to the bells I had heard arriving here.

I quickly sat up and the bell stopped, I wasn't sure how long I had been asleep, but I knew it wasn't long as I was still tired. My stomach rumbled and I remembered what the sound of the bell meant; it was time for food. Using a lot of magic made you hungrier so I knew I needed to eat. I got up and wondered over to the sink, then splashed some water onto my face, I glanced up at the mirror above the sink and noticed my eye was still red so I rubbed it hoping it would turn brown again, it didn't.

Last time this had happened it had gone back to normal once I had rested but not this time. I sighed out loud and rubbed it again, having one eye red made me look evil.

Then I suddenly heard a familiar voice, "**Don't worry Rose, you still look pretty.**"

"Thank you Lucas.... Wait.... Lucas!" I stared into the mirror, but I could not see his reflection.

"Lucas, can you hear me?" I asked.

"**Of course I can, I'm standing right here.**" He replied.

I walked back into the bedroom and there he was, standing in front of the door, but I could also see

29

the door through him, I slowly walked over to him and held my hand out to touch him, Lucas smiled and raised his hand to reach mine, our fingers touched but then my hand went through his.

"A ghost." I whispered.

"We haven't seen each other in a while and that's what you say to me, that's not very nice you know." He said.

I slowly stepped back and looked down at the jewel around my neck, but it wasn't glowing, I suddenly felt weak, so I sat down on the floor.

"Maybe I'm still dreaming." I said quietly and looked back up at Lucas.

Lucas laughed **"That's what you said when we first met, and my answer is the same. You're not dreaming, you are awake."**

He walked over, no he floated towards me and knelt down beside me.

I smiled at him and said, "So I guess it's magic."

"Yep."

"But how am I seeing you like this? Before it was just through reflections, and in my dreams."

"I am not sure; I'm guessing it is because you're at my home now. I feel stronger and I have more of a connection here, and your magic has gotten stronger too. I'm just happy I can talk to you again." He replied.

Tears welled up in my eyes, "Me too, I missed you a lot."

"I missed you too, don't cry."

I rubbed my eyes and asked, "Where did you go before, why did I stop seeing you?"

"I don't know, I felt like I was still near you and the jewel, but I couldn't talk to you anymore. As soon as you got to Sunlight City, I felt myself getting stronger again and I have more of a connection to the magic around us, then I heard your wish that you wanted to see me again, so I took this form. I would have talked to you sooner, but you fell asleep." He smiled.

I nodded as I took in what he had said, then my stomach rumbled.
　　"Go get some food, you definitely need it." Laughed Lucas.
　　"What about you, you won't leave again will you?"
　　"I will be fine; I will stay for as long as I can. You will see me around, just call my name when you need me." He replied.

"Alright, do you think I should tell the others I can see you again?"
　　"If you need to you can, but I would prefer you didn't. It might upset them again and I think Tristan is finally getting on with his life instead of blaming himself, I just want him to be happy." Explained Lucas.

"OK I won't tell them; you really are the best big brother." I smiled.
　　"Thank you Rose, now hurry up and go get some food before the others eat it all."
　　"Alright I'm going, see you later Lucas." I said as I opened the door.

"Bye Rose."
I closed the door behind me then headed towards the stairs; I walked slowly as I was thinking about what had just happened. I was glad I could see Lucas again but also scared, my magic was getting stronger I could feel it every day and also Lucas wasn't the first ghost I had seen.

I had also seen one at Greenfield Village, the boy who I had killed accidentally with my magic, Caleb. He had appeared one day while I had been practicing using my magic, he said he was going to haunt me for the rest of my life and for some reason he still wanted me to join the Dark Shadow Guild.
I hadn't seen him here yet though and I hadn't told anyone about it, I didn't want to worry them and seeing ghosts cannot be a good sign.

As I walked back down the spiral staircase I realized I had not looked at the map to find out where the cafeteria was, but I remembered Isabella had said it was on the first floor, so I kept going down. There was no one else on the stairs but I could hear voices below me, I glanced down over the railing and my eyes zoomed in to focus, I could see people in the small garden sat on benches around small tables and I noticed they were eating.
Instead of going to the other staircase on the second floor where Odin's office was, I stayed on the spiral staircase and made it to the first floor. It was busy in the entrance hall, Mystical Knights and Kings Guards walked about or stood in groups chatting. I noticed a few of them look my way, I smiled at them and followed my nose to the

cafeteria.

I pushed open the large double doors and walked in, the room was huge and full of people sat at many tables eating, drinking, talking, and laughing together.

I headed towards the back of the room where I could see people queuing up waiting to be served some food, but before I got there I noticed Tristan back in his human form sat at a large table, eating and talking with some men, some were wearing the red Kings Guards uniforms, but I noticed a few with orange cloaks on. I remember reading in a book the members of the Mystic Council wore the orange cloaks, I started to walk over to the table but then stopped as it looked like they were having an important conversation and I wasn't sure if I was allowed to sit next to the prince.

I decided to get some food first, but as I stood in the queue I heard whispers, people were talking about the jewel of darkness and I heard one girl say it was a curse to get near the one carrying it, so I changed my mind and decided I would come back later for food, when everyone else had left. I quickly turned around to leave and crashed straight into Edmund.

"Hello Rose, I hope you weren't leaving without saying anything to me."

I laughed and gave Edmund a hug "Hello Ed, it's good to see you again."

"Now that's better, come on lets get you some food I bet your hungry after putting up that magic shield." He said and turned me back around towards the food table.

As the others in the queue had left we walked straight up to the table that was covered in all different types of food, it looked and smelled delicious.

"Go on dig in, take as much as you want." Said Edmund and he handed me a tray.

A large man wearing an apron, and I somehow knew he could change into a bear, came over with a tray of hot pies and put them on the table.
   "Ah, Carson I will take some of them, this is my friend Rose she likes to eat too." Said Edmund as he grabbed two pies off the plate.
   "Hello, Welcome to Sunrise Tower. I'm Carson Cox the chef, please take what you need and if there is anything I can cook for you please let me know." He said.

"It's nice to meet you, all the food looks lovely thank you." I said and grabbed two pies too and poured myself a glass of water from a jug.
   "Come on Rose we can go sit over there." Said Edmund and he walked off towards a table where three tall men in red uniforms were sat.
And I noticed one was a shapeshifter; he was also a bear.
   "Hey Ed, is this your friend you were telling us about?" Said one of the men as he pushed his glasses up his nose and looked at me.

I looked at Edmund and he laughed, "Don't worry I have only told them good stories about you. This is Hector, Aaron, and Ryan they are Kings Guards. This is Rose." He told the men as he sat down opposite them.

"Hello, it's nice to meet you." I said and sat down next to Edmund.

"Hello." All three of them said at once.

We all laughed, and the boys started to eat their food, I grabbed a pie and dug in. Yum.

"So Rose is it true, did you put up that magic shield outside?" Asked Aaron.

I nodded.

"That's crazy, I've never seen one that big before, how long will it stay up?" Asked Hector.

I gulped down some water shocked, "It's still up around the castle?"

"Not just around the castle, it covered all of Sunlight City." Said Hector.

"Yeah Edmund was right, you are strong." Said Ryan the bear shapeshifter.

I glanced at Edmund, and he shrugged.

The entire city and it was still up! Last time I had used this magic it had only lasted a few minutes and Greenfield Village was a lot smaller than Sunlight City, no wonder I was still tired.

"I am not sure how long it will stay up; it normally just disappears on its own." I explained.

"Oh right, well it will keep us safer. I guess it makes our job easier too." Smiled Ryan.

"Yeah, maybe the captain will give us the night off." Laughed Hector.

I smiled then I heard someone shout, "Rose."

I turned around in my seat and saw Clover and Marigold coming towards us.

35

The three guards stood up and saluted, I looked at them puzzled.

Edmund laughed and said, "Marigold and Clover are basically fairy princesses, so the guards have to salute or bow when they go near them."
   "Hey, you're supposed to do it too." Said Ryan.
"Don't be silly none of you need to do that, we are Mystical Knights too." Said Marigold.

Oh, right I forgot, Marigold and Clover are the fairy queen's nieces. They both sat down next to me.

"Thank you for saving me earlier Rose." Said Marigold.
   I nodded and asked, "How is your arm?" It was wrapped up in a large bandage.
   "The medic said it's just a small fracture, but it will take a few weeks to heal, so I won't be flying any time soon." She said sadly.

"I thought that party was tonight though." Said Edmund.
   "Party?" Asked Aaron.
"Yes, there is an important fairy ball happening tonight, but you have to be in your fairy form to go. So, we won't be able to go now." Explained Clover.
   "I told you; you can still go." Sighed Marigold.
"No, I'm not leaving you alone and it won't be fun without you there." Said Clover.

Marigold smiled at her younger sister. I knew there was a way I could help her, but I couldn't tell Marigold because I knew she wouldn't agree.

So, I held out my hand and touched hers and said, "Don't worry."

Marigold's eyes grew wide as she realized what I was doing, my magic absorbed her pain and injury and transferred it over to me.
I yelled out as my arm cracked; Marigold was healed but still the only way for me to heal others was to take the damage myself.

"You idiot, you should never have done that!" Shouted Marigold.
  "I'm confused, what happened?" Asked Hector.
"Rose has healed me but now she is hurt." Replied Marigold angrily.

I took a deep breath as I felt dizzy. I still hadn't recovered from using my magic before, maybe I should have waited, I thought.

"Rose, are you alright?"
I looked up into bright green eyes, Tristan had felt my pain through our mind link. The guards quickly stood up and saluted again.

I nodded and smiled, "Don't worry, I found out before that I heal fast like a shapeshifter, I will be fine in a couple of days and now you can go to the party." I said and looked back at Marigold.

"You think I care more about a party than my friends health!" Shouted Marigold.
  "No, but…."
Marigold got up and stormed out of the cafeteria and Clover chased after her.

"It's alright Rose, Marigold is only worried about you she will calm down soon, but next time don't put yourself at risk. We don't like seeing you hurt." Said Edmund.

I sighed and tried to move my arm which caused me to hiss out in pain.

"Come on Rose, you're coming with me." Said Tristan and he took hold of my uninjured arm and dragged me to my feet.
  "Bye." I called out to the others as Tristan led me away.

We left the cafeteria, and I noticed two Kings Guards who I hadn't met yet were following us, they were both tall and looked strong. They also had bright yellow eyes and somehow, I knew straight away they were wolves.
I realized who they were, Jaxon and Gray, Tristan's special guards who had been chosen to stay by his side and help him while he was acting prince. I had spoken with them before when I had called Tristan on my S.C.D. while I was still living at Unicorn Stables.

"Hello Rose, it's nice to finally meet you in person, I'm Jaxon the handsome one and that's Gray." Said Jaxon as he saw me looking at them.
  Gray shook his head and waved at me, I smiled but before I could say anything to them, I was pulled through another door that was opposite the cafeteria.
  "Wait outside." Said Tristan to Jaxon and Gray.

He then took me over to a large desk where a fairy

with silver eyes and short pink hair tied up in two braids was sat reading a book, she glanced up, then shot to her feet.

"Ah, Prince Tristan. What can I help you with, you aren't hurt are you?" She asked as she curtsied.

"Hello Summer, no I'm alright but my friend Rose has hurt her arm please can you help her?" Replied Tristan.

She looked at me and smiled, "Of course I can, that is my job. Please take a seat on one of the empty beds, I will be with you in a minute I have to check another patient first." She said then hurried behind a curtain to another bed.

I glanced at Tristan, and he smiled and dragged me to one of the empty beds, we both sat down, and I looked around the room. It had a few beds with curtains hanging around them, cupboards and shelves along the opposite wall that were stacked with medical books and supplies and there was a small office at the back of the room, I guess this must be the medical room.

I sighed out loud, I didn't want to be examined I would have just bandaged up my arm myself.

"Don't give me that look Rose, it's your own fault." Smiled Tristan.

"I told you I will be fine in a few days you don't need to fuss, at least it's not broken this time." I said as I rubbed my arm.

"Broken, so you have done this before?" Asked Tristan.

I nodded, "A few months ago Hannah fell off her horse and broke her arm, I didn't like seeing her in

39

pain and the jewel must have reacted to my feelings when I gave her a hug, I healed her but got a broken arm myself, it hurt a lot more than this. The Unicorn members were not happy and made me rest for weeks, they wouldn't let me do anything and it drove me nuts. As the doctor visited me, we both realized I heal faster than humans, it was a big shock to Doctor Thomas. Lucas said I heal fast just like shapeshifters, but we don't know how, as it hasn't happened to anyone with the jewel before, he said I must be special." I smiled.

"I see. I wish you would have told me; I would have visited you."
   "I didn't want to worry you and anyway you had your own problems to deal with, the prince of Sunlight City couldn't exactly run off to Greenfield Village." I replied and smiled.

"I would have; it would have given me a much-needed break from all the boring meetings I had to have with the Mystic Council."
   "Trust me, the way some people acted afterwards would have given you an even bigger headache." I said, as I remembered the cues of injured people lining up to get healed by the miracle magic user as the rumors had spread to nearby villages about my magic, but once I told them I couldn't heal the sick, and some of the injured people whose injuries were too bad or had been that way a while, their angry faces still haunted me.

"Why, what happened?" Asked Tristan with a look of concern.

Before I could answer him Summer came over to us and said, "Right, lets get you fixed up shall we." I nodded, and gently rolled up the long sleeve of my top.

"Let me check what's wrong first." Said Summer and held out her hand over my arm.

"It's fractured just like Marigold's was, so I just need it wrapping up." I explained.

She looked at me confused then touched my arm, I could feel the warm light of her magic as she checked my injury. Some fairies have a gift that lets them check injuries, wounds, and sickness with their magic by touch, I had not seen it before, but I knew Clover now had the ability too. Most fairies that had this magic skill became doctors and nurses.

"You are right, it's the exact same injury but how did you know, how did this happen?" She asked as her bright silver eyes widened in shock.

"Rose healed Marigold with her magic but got her injury instead." Explained Tristan.

"Wow really, I've never heard of that magic before." Said Summer.

"What magic are we talking about?" Said a tall slim man as he walked towards us.

He had dark brown hair and eyes, and I knew he was human; he bowed at Tristan then looked at me and smiled.

"This is Rose, she healed Marigold's arm but now she has her injury. Her arm is fractured in the exact same place." Explained Summer.

"Really! How fascinating, I'm Doctor Wesley

White. It's nice to meet you." He said.

"Hello." I said and smiled.

"Oh Tristan, Gray said you have to be somewhere. Don't worry about your friend we will take care of her." Said the Doctor.

"Right, I will see you later Rose. Stay out of trouble." Said Tristan and he walked to the door.

"Ok, you too." I smiled.

Before he left, he opened our mind link and said, **"And later you can tell me what happened at Greenfield Village."**

"Alright fine." I replied.

He smiled and waved then left the room.

As Summer got to work wrapping my arm up Doctor Wesley asked me some questions.

"So, are you a fairy, how do you heal others?" He asked and looked into my eyes. My red eye must be confusing him.

"No, I'm human but I have this, it lets me use magic." I explained and pointed to the jewel around my neck.

"The jewel of darkness!" Gasped Summer as she finally noticed the jewel.

"Ah so you're the new girl I have some medical forms you need to fill in, but first can I ask, can you heal any injury with that?" Asked Doctor Wesley.

"I'm not sure, I've healed a broken arm and a few cuts but the only way for me to heal someone is for me to take the damage myself, so I don't do it often. And I can't heal myself, but I heal faster than humans like the shapeshifters." I smiled.

"Interesting, I don't think I've heard of a magic like

this either. I know some fairies can help with wounds and illnesses but not in the way you do. Next time it happens would it be alright if we run some tests to see how your body heals afterwards."

Tests, I wasn't sure I liked the sound of that.
    "Don't worry Rose, the doctor is kind, he isn't a mad scientist he won't do anything you don't want him to." Smiled Summer.
    The Doctor laughed, "Yes my curiosity makes me sound crazy sometimes, but I just want to learn all I can, so I can help more people. I understand if you don't want to though, but maybe I can find out how you heal others so you can learn how to heal yourself too."

"Alright, I guess I would also like to know how my magic works." I said and looked down at the jewel.
    "Excellent, oh but try not to get hurt. I don't want to see that, and I don't want the prince to get angry at me." He smiled.

"Right, you're all done Rose, try not to use your arm too much and come back here if it is causing you any more pain. I would like to see you again sometime next week so I can check how its healing and change your bandage if needed." Said Summer.

I nodded and checked the bandage; it was wrapped up well.
"Well, I better go and check my other patients, you take care Rose, and remember if you ever feel unwell or get hurt come to us anytime." Said Doctor Wesley and he walked off towards his

office.

 "Alright, thank you." I said and stood up to leave.

"Would you like any Calendula tea before you go? It will help with the pain." Asked Summer.

 Calendula is a special plant the fairies can make into tea and ointments that helps relieve pain and sometimes cures certain illnesses.

"No, it's alright, thank you Summer." I replied.

 "Your welcome and thank you for healing our princess, goodbye." She smiled and followed Doctor Wesley into his office.

"Bye." I said and left the room.

Chapter 5.
New Uniform.

Once I left the medical room I headed back outside the tower, outside I took a deep breath and breathed in the cool fresh air then I looked up and noticed the rain had stopped and my magical shield had gone, and I wondered if it vanished once I had used my magic to heal Marigold.

I shrugged and decided to head in the direction of the stables as I wanted to make sure Silver was settling into his new home, and as Clover had chased after Marigold earlier, I hadn't had the chance to ask her how he was doing.
As I walked, I noticed how immaculate the grounds were, and the different colored flowers and plants sparkled in the sun that had appeared out from behind the clouds. I also noticed some Kings Guards out on patrol they glanced at me and continued walking past.

The horse stables came into view, and you could tell a king owned them as there were huge and stunning, I bet the horses loved living here and I hoped Silver would too.
I headed through the gate to find Silver; I couldn't see him in the stables, but I noticed a stable boy mucking out, so I walked over to him.
"Hello, I'm looking for my horse." I said.

The boy stopped working and looked up, his light blue eyes grew wide as he looked at me.
"Hello, is that the jewel of darkness, are you the one who put up that magic shield before?" He

asked.

"Yes, to both questions." I smiled.

"Wow, cool. My name is Ethan Knox, I will show you to the fields where some of the horses are, your horse will be there with my sister." He said, then he put down the fork and held his hand out for me to shake.

"Thank you, I'm Rose Ashley." I replied as I shook his hand.

He led me back through the gate and asked, "So what's your horse called?"

"Silver, Clover brought him here earlier." I replied. "Ah right, yes, I remember. The horse with the silver eyes, don't worry he is settling in fine. I promised Clover I would take good care of him." He said and blushed.

It looks like Clover has an admirer; I smiled and nodded.

We got to a large field, and I could see many horses all grazing on the grass, a young girl was stood at the gate watching them.

"Hey sis." Shouted Ethan.

The girl turned around, and I noticed she had the same blond hair and blue eyes as her brother. "This is Leah, she helped put your horse in the field." Said Ethan, then he turned to Leah and said, "This is Rose, she wants to know how her horse Silver is doing."

"Hello." I said.

"Hello, Silver is alright he's a good boy, though he did nearly bite the new stable assistant. He should be around here somewhere." She said then looked back at the horses.

"He did? That's weird he doesn't normally bite." I said and looked into the field; I spotted Silver near the trees at the back eating some grass.

"It's alright, he is probably just getting used to all the new faces and even I'm not that keen on Declan." Explained Ethan.
"Ethan don't be rude." Said Leah.
Ethan stuck out his tongue and then smiled at me. I laughed and asked, "Would it be alright if I go and see him."

"Yes of course, he's your horse, you can see him whenever you want. Just make sure you shut the gate, if the horses escape again, we will be in trouble." Said Ethan.
"Don't say that. Don't worry Rose that was a long time ago and it hasn't happened since." Said Leah.

"It's alright, Silver will stay close even if he escapes which he will probably start doing once he settles in, he likes to go on walks, so if he does go missing don't worry, he will come back when he is ready." I explained.
"Thanks for telling us, we will tell the stable manager, so he doesn't think we lost a horse." Smiled Ethan.
"Thank you." I said to them both then I opened the gate and walked through.

As soon as Leah shut the gate behind me, I saw Silver lift his head up and as he recognized me, he started to trot towards me.

"Hello boy, do you like your new home?"

I laughed as he nuzzled my hair, then he neighed, and I knew he was happy. I have always been able to understand how he is feeling and what he wants, but it's not just with Silver, I can understand all animals, my mother always said it was a gift I inherited from my father. Though I never knew my father, so I wasn't sure if it was true.
As I was stroking Silver on his neck, I sensed another horse approaching us, I turned around and smiled as I recognized the horse, it was Patrick, Tristan's horse and he also looked happy to see me.

"Hello Patrick." I said and gave him a pat as he nuzzled my hands looking for treats.

I remembered I still had peppermints in the pouch on my belt, so I gave one to Silver and one to Patrick.

"Alright you two I can only give you one, you don't want to get fat. I better go before the other horses find out, you two be good I will see you tomorrow." I said and patted them both on the neck before I turned to leave.

As I got back to the gate, I noticed two men watching me.

"Hello, you must be Rose?" The older man asked.

"Hello, yes I'm Rose." I replied and he opened the gate for me, but he had to quickly shut it behind me as Silver was also coming out.

"Whoa, not you boy, you need to stay with the other horses." He said.

"Silver, I said be good, go back to Patrick." I laughed.

Silver huffed turned back around and made his way back over the field to where Patrick was waiting.

"My name is George Wells and I'm the stable manager, I was going to say if you need any help with your horse we are here to help you, but it doesn't look like you need us. You must have a close bond with your horse for him to listen to you like that." Said the older man as he rubbed his short black beard.

"Thank you, yes, we are very close but if Silver causes you any trouble, please let me know. I know he can be a handful sometimes." I said, then looked at the other man who had stayed quiet and was watching me. He looked younger than George, but he was bald, and he had a mean looking snake tattoo on his head.

"This is Declan Pike, the new stable assistant, so if you need anything come to me or him, don't worry he is nicer than he looks." George laughed.

Declan gave George an annoyed look then looked at me and said, "Hello."

"Hello." I said and smiled.

For some reason I felt uneasy around him, something seemed off, I couldn't work out what it was, but I felt like I couldn't trust him. Maybe that's why Silver had tried to bite him, before I could work out what was wrong, Ethan ran up to us.

"Some more Kings Guards are back from patrol; we need help with the horses." He said.

"Right, we better get back to work, see you later Rose." Said George.

"Bye." I replied.

Ethan waved as he followed him back towards the stables, Declan nodded at me then left with them. I watched them leave then I looked back at Silver one last time before I headed back towards the tower.

As I got back to the steps of the tower, I heard someone shout my name.

"Rose." Shouted Marigold.

I turned back around, and she stopped in front of me.

"I'm sorry I shouted at you before, thank you for healing my arm." She said.

"You don't have to apologize I understand you were just worried, I'm just glad you're alright now." I replied.

"Yeah just don't do it again, I don't want to see you get hurt."

"I can't make any promises." I laughed.

Marigold smiled then said, "Come on, I'm on my way to the seamstress you should come too, you need to be fitted for your uniforms."

"Ok." I said and followed her back inside the tower.

We climbed the many stairs to the fourth floor and got to room five. The red door had a sign that read 'Washing room - Seamstress Vivian Lowell.' Marigold knocked on the door and a woman's voice shouted "Come in."

We both walked through the door, once inside I noticed many clothes hung up around the room and the two washing boxes on one side of the room, these boxes were powered by light stones and were used to wash clothes and bedding.
At the back of the room was a desk full of material and sewing equipment and a woman with bright purple hair was sat behind the desk sewing, she looked up at us as we approached.

"Hello Vivian, this is Rose. She has come to get fitted for her new student uniform." Said Marigold.
  "Hello." I said.
"Ah yes hello, I've been expecting you. Please stand over here." She said and pointed to a space behind her desk.

I stood still as Vivian got a tape measurer and started taking my measurements, she wrote down the numbers then walked over to a rail of clothes and started looking through them.
  "Ah, here we go." She said and grabbed a green uniform off the rail.

"As you can see, the student uniform is a dark green color and when you become a Mystical Knight you will then get to wear the blue uniform. The Kings Guards uniforms are red, the color of the uniforms help the people understand who they go to for any assistance they may need. As you are human you don't need the thinner uniforms the shapeshifters get, they need them so they can remove their clothes easier to transform and I can easily repair them when needed. This one should fit you, please change over there and I can make any adjustments if needed." Vivian explained and handed me the uniform.

When the Mystical Knight's had stayed at
Greenfield Village they had not worn their uniforms
as they had wanted to stay undercover in the non-
magic realm and technically they were also on
holiday, so it was good to be able to see the
uniforms now, I had only seen them on a photo
Odin had shown me.
I walked behind the curtain she had pointed at, so
I could change into my new uniform.
The only difference between the Mystical Knight,
student uniform and the Kings Guard uniform was
the color of the jacket and the name under the
crest.
My jacket was the dark green of the student
uniform and on the front was the king's crest. The
crest was a growling tiger's head on a shield to
represent the shapeshifter king, there was also a
crown above the tiger's head and above that a sun
with eagle wings attached to both sides, also
above the ears of the tiger was a small paw print
and horse shoe, to honor the many animals under
the care of the shapeshifter king, it read 'Student'
under the crest.
The trousers were black with an orange stripe
down the sides of each leg and the black tee shirt
was plain with an orange stripe around each
sleeve.

As I dressed I could hear Vivian and Marigold
talking about the dress Marigold was going to
wear at tonight's fairy ball. I had to take care
putting on my tee shirt and jacket due to my
injured arm but once I was dressed I looked in the
large mirror on the wall and smiled, even though I

wasn't a Mystical Knight yet, the uniform made me
feel like one, but the sleeves would need some
adjusting as they were a bit long.

I walked back around the curtain and Marigold
said, "You look great Rose."
 "Thanks." I laughed and waved my sleeve.
"Right, let's get you pinned up." Said Vivian and
she grabbed a pot of pins off her desk and got to
work pinning up the sleeves of my jacket and the
waist of my trousers as they also felt loose.

Once she finished that, she grabbed a belt off
another railing.
 "Here, now try this on and I will get you your
cloak, hat and gloves."

I wrapped the sword belt around my waist, and I
noticed there was also a small pouch and the
holder for my dagger attached to it.
Vivian then handed me a pair of black gloves that
had orange stripes around the wrists and a long
brown winter cloak that also had the king's crest
on the back.

"Here try this on too, it should fit." She said and
handed me a hat.
I put it on my head, and it fit well.
 "Good, that's alright, you only need to wear your
hat on special occasions like at parties or big
meetings, on certain missions and if you ever have
an audience with a member of the royal family."
Explained Vivian.

"Don't worry Rose, you don't need to wear it if you
go and visit Tristan, unless he is inside the castle

then you may need it, but not many get to go in there anyway." Said Marigold.

"Ah yes it is a shame, we used to go to lovely parties at the castle. The ball room is very grand, and I loved making the beautiful dresses for the late queen and her guests but sadly that doesn't happen anymore, hopefully once the king settles down with his new girlfriend, we can start attending parties again, I would love to make the dresses again, I've just been making boring uniforms." Sighed Vivian.

"Alright Vivian, next time I go to a fairy ball I will let you design and make my dress." Said Marigold.

"Really! Oh, thank you Marigold." Said Vivian and she gave Marigold a hug.

"Ok calm down, I think Rose is missing something." Laughed Marigold and she pointed down at my feet.

"Ah yes, you are right, what size shoe do you wear?" Asked Vivian.

"Normally a size five." I replied.

She nodded, ran to a cupboard, and pulled out a box.

"Right, try these on." She said and handed me the box.

I pulled out a pair of long black boots, they also had the orange stripe around the top of them and laces down one of the sides. I pulled them on, and they fit perfectly, they were comfortable and would be good to ride in.

"Yeah, they are fine." I said.

"Good, you can choose them to wear, but I would recommend your shoes for now due to the warmer weather, take your boots, the cloak, hat, and gloves now and I will adjust the rest and get them sent to your room tomorrow morning, along with your shoes and tracksuit you will need for your fitness training. They should get to you just before you leave for breakfast and your first lesson." Said Vivian.

"Thank you."
   "No need to thank me, it's my job and if you need any help with your clothes and if you need anything mending, please come to me. I hope you will like your new home Rose." She said.
   "I'm sure I will." I nodded and smiled.

"Come on then Rose, you better get back to your room and get some more rest. You have a big day tomorrow you have your first lessons." Said Marigold.

Once I had changed back into my normal clothes I headed back to my room with Marigold.
We stopped at my door and Marigold said, "Well I better go and find Clover so we can both get ready for the fairy ball, remember your schedule for tomorrow and the rest of the week is in your diary so have a look at that. And don't worry about the lessons you will be fine, thank you again for fixing my arm. See you tomorrow."

"Ok, thank you for your help. Bye." I said and waved at her as she headed off down the corridor.

I then entered my room and shut the door behind me.

Chapter 6.

Appearance of an Os-yen and meeting students.

I was in a dark forest, shadow demons appeared all around me. I felt lost, alone, and afraid. Out of the darkness Caleb appeared and I shot him with a blast of magic, he turned to dust, and I heard a girl scream. Then a large snake appeared, and I heard knocking.

Knock, knock, knock.
I suddenly woke up and it took me a while to remember where I was, knock, knock.

"Miss Rose Ashley are you in there? I have a delivery for you." Shouted a boy.

I quickly jumped out of bed and wrapped my blanket around me then patted down my messed-up hair before I opened the door.

"Good morning, here you go. A parcel from Vivian the seamstress." Said a small boy who looked about twelve years old. The name tag on his jacket read 'Matthew Hill.'

I didn't take the box off him though as something caught my eye beside him. I stared, blinked my eyes, and stared again and I wondered if I was still asleep.

"It's rude to stare." Said the giant rabbit that was stood beside Matthew.
 "Um...." I replied.
The large brown and white rabbit would be about

the size of a large cat when stood on all four legs but as he was stood up onto his back legs he was nearly as tall as Matthew. I watched in awe as the rabbit pulled something out of the small pouch that was tied around his waist.

"Here, please sign this." He said and held out a small card and pen.
   When I didn't move, he shouted, "Come on we haven't got all day, I want to go and get my carrot."
   "I'm guessing this is the first delivery rabbit you have seen." Laughed Matthew.
   "Yes, I'm sorry I didn't mean to stare; I've read books about delivery rabbits but it's different seeing one in front of me."

A delivery rabbit is a breed of rabbit called Os-yen. These rabbits can talk and walk on its back legs when it wanted to, they could also use their front paws to carry objects. These rabbits decided to become delivery rabbits many years ago so they could help out the shapeshifter king. These days they also make deliveries for others with the help of children and get paid with money and food, so they can live in peace with their families.

I took the card and pen off the rabbit and signed my name on the dotted line under Vivian's name, so they had proof I had received the package.
   "I'm Rose, it is nice to meet you both." I smiled and handed the card and pen back to the rabbit.
   "Well, we know that, we wouldn't be here if you weren't." Said the rabbit.
   "Don't mind him, the grumpy rabbit is Alba and I'm Matthew."

I smiled and took the box off him.
"Thank you Matthew and Alba." I said.

"Your welcome, if you need any letters or parcels
delivered to anyone please come to us. We live in
the burrow just past the stables." Said Matthew,
then he waved and walked back down the
corridor.
Alba's nose twitched then he got back down on all
four legs.
    "Bye." He said and hopped off after Matthew.
"Goodbye." I replied and watched them leave.

I looked down at the large box in my hand and
remembered Vivian had said she would have my
uniform delivered to me before breakfast, I just
didn't realize a boy and a rabbit would be the one
to deliver it.
I guess that's another thing I will have to get used
to in my new life at Sunlight City. I smiled and
walked back into my bedroom, once the door was
shut I opened the box.
My uniform and tracksuit was inside with a note
from Vivian that read, 'Dear Rose, here are your new
clothes. I hope it all fits you well, if you have any
problems, please come back to me so I can fix them. I
have also included a welcome gift, a new ribbon to tie
up your lovely hair. I hope you do well in your training
to become a Mystical Knight. Love Vivian.'

I smiled, took the light blue ribbon from the box,
and tied up my long auburn hair into a braid. As I
had looked at my schedule last night I knew I
needed to put on my tracksuit as I would be at the
training yard before breakfast for my fitness and
weapons training lesson with the teacher Dominic

Nash.

Once I had changed into my tracksuit I looked in the mirror, the tracksuit was the same dark green color as the uniform jacket, and it also had the king's crest on the front. It fit well, even with my bandaged arm and it was comfortable and so were the soft black shoes I had found at the bottom of the box.

I was annoyed my eye was still red and I wondered if it would ever get back to normal, maybe I should go and ask the doctor about it later, I thought.

I opened up my diary and folded out the map of the grounds, the training yard was behind the tower near the gate that led to the nearby forest behind the wall. I should be able to find it just fine, so I folded the map back up and placed my diary inside the pouch that was attached to my new belt, then I headed out.

Once outside I headed towards the training yard, they were more Mystical Knights and Kings Guards outside today and everyone seemed in high spirits. I heard a lot of shouting and laughing in the direction of the training yard and as I walked people smiled and waved at me and a few said hello as they walked past.

I got to the training yard and suddenly spotted Lucas floating near the fence, he waved at me and pointed towards two boys fighting with swords in the arena and I realized it was Tristan and Edmund practicing. I stood beside Lucas and watched them; it looked like Edmund had improved a lot since I last saw him train and Tristan was great as always.

As I watched them, I wondered if I could beat the boys now as I had improved a lot too thanks to my lessons with Sophia; a woman I had made friends with when she had visited Greenfield Village. She is one of the best sword fighters I have seen, and she may be able to even beat Odin. She had given me a katana sword as a gift and taught me how to use it better than a knightly sword.

I sensed someone approaching so I turned around and saw a tall muscular man, he had his black hair tied in a small bun on top of his head he also had yellow eyes, and I knew he was a wolf shapeshifter.

"So, you must be the new student, Rose, was it?" He said in a deep voice.

"Hello, yes I'm Rose Ashley." I replied.
"Hello, I'm Dominic Nash and I will be your fitness and weapons teacher. I heard you had injured your arm, how is it feeling today?" He asked.

"It's alright, it's getting better." I replied and rubbed the bandage under my sleeve.

"Good, luckily for you we aren't training with our weapons today. The other students are gathering over there, lets go and join them." He said and walked off towards the group gathered near the gate.

Before I could follow him, I heard a voice in my head, "**Good luck Rose.**" Said Tristan.
I looked back at him and saw him and Edmund waving at me, I smiled and waved back, then I quickly followed Dominic, Lucas also followed us.

The group of students were stood in front of the gate that led to the forest, they were all happily talking to each other and laughing but once they spotted us, they went quiet.

"Good, now that everyone is here, I would like you all to meet our new student Rose Ashley, please introduce yourselves one at a time." Said Dominic.

I had heard there was six other students who were training to become Mystical Knights, and they had started their training earlier than me.
    "Hi I'm Yara Jett." Said a tall girl with long black hair, she was a human like me.
    "Hello, I'm Jasper Moore." Said another wolf shapeshifter.
    "Good morning Rose, my name is Iris Crow, I hope we can become good friends." Smiled the fairy with short black hair and purple eyes.
    "Hi Rose, I'm Joseph Ross." Said a tall boy with short blonde hair.
    "I'm Ted Jason but you can call me T.J." Nodded a strong looking boy with dark orange eyes and somehow I knew he could change into a bear.
    "Does anyone know where Liv is?" Asked Dominic.
    "Yes, she said she was going to ask the medic about something." Answered Iris.
    "Very well, we will start without her, today's lesson will help your fitness and stamina. We will be carrying these heavy bags on your back through the forest to a cart at the check point and you will be running, everyone grab a bag." Explained Dominic and he picked up one of the bags.

We all took a bag from the pile and strapped them to our backs; Dominic helped me put mine on as

he had seen me struggling with my bad arm.
As we did this, I noticed the other students staring
at my neck and I looked down and noticed the
jewel was glowing a light blue, it must have
sensed I was nervous. I took a deep breath and
concentrated on Dominic as he handed me a
small map, the other students already had one
and I noticed them double checking it to make
sure they knew the route we were going to take.
Dominic unclipped the S.C.D. from his belt and
spoke into it.
"Summer, if Liv is alright can you send her back to
my lesson and tell her to carry the bag I will leave
at the gate through the forest to the check point
and tell her to run if she can."
 He nodded as he listened to Summer's reply and
then said, "Yes Ok, thanks."

Dominic then turned back to us and said, "Right,
you all should remember where the check point is
but if you have forgotten it is marked on your
maps, we will be running together today as we
have Rose with us and she is unfamiliar with the
forest but if any of you want to run faster you can,
lets go."

The Kings Guard that was stood at the gate wrote
our names down on a clipboard and we all walked
through the gate and entered the forest.
Dominic led our group further into the forest then
he started to jog and the rest of us followed him.

As we ran, I kept looking down at the map in my
hand to try and remember the way we had come.
This forest was bigger than the one at Greenfield
Village and it felt older too, there was also a lot

more different types of plants and trees.

The other students were good at running and were keeping up with Dominic well, I was at the back of the group as I have never been good at long distant running, and I normally just jumped on Silver if I ever had to travel far. I guess I would need to train more.

I noticed Jasper and T.J. decided to overtake Dominic and it looked like they had decided to have a race, the other students laughed and picked up the pace with Dominic who had sped up. I should have known training with shapeshifters wasn't going to be easy. I glanced back down at the map and noticed we were getting closer to the check point, which was good as I felt my energy getting low, having nightmares throughout the night again had not helped.

We finally made it to the cart and Jasper and T.J. were sat waiting.

"What took you so long?" Said Jasper with a smile.

"Thank you for volunteering to load up the cart, everyone give your bags to Jasper and T.J." said Dominic and he threw his bag at Jasper and smiled.

As everyone started to take their bags off their backs and give them to the boys I bent down and tried to catch my breath.

"Are you alright Rose?" Asked Dominic with concern.

"Yes, sorry." I replied and started to un-strap my bag.

"There is no need to apologize you did well, when the other humans started their training, I had to keep stopping to make sure they were still standing." Smiled Dominic as he helped me pull my bag over my bad arm.

"Hey, we heard that!" Shouted Joseph.
Everyone laughed and I smiled and handed my bag to T.J. as he had held his hand out towards me.

"Thank you." I said.

"Right, this cart will be picked up by some Mystical Knights and they will be taking the supplies to a lookout tower in the mountains. Moving supplies around to different locations is another part of the many jobs Mystical Knights have to complete, so you have to keep your fitness up the best you can, to manage some of the heavy bags. Sometimes we will do this alone and other times as a group, so it is also important you all learn to work as a team. Now we will have a short break before we start running back to the tower for breakfast." Explained Dominic.

We all sat down on the side of the cart to have a rest, and for a while we listened as Dominic explained why there was a lookout tower in the mountains, but as he told the story something didn't feel right, and I felt a dark presence near us. I heard a rustle in the trees, and I suddenly saw a dark shape closing in. A shadow demon!

I fired some magic off towards it and I heard a girl scream.

"Rose! What are you doing?" Shouted Dominic.
I looked back at the spot where I saw the shadow demon and saw a girl with light brown hair lying face down on the ground. The other students ran

over to her and helped pick her up off the ground. "Why did you fire at me?" She shouted with a red angry face.

The other students also looked mad, and I also noticed fear in their eyes.
   "I'm sorry, I…..I thought I saw a shadow demon!" I explained.
   "The only demon around here is you; I could have died!" She cried.
   "Enough Liv. Rose you should not use your magic like that, even if you did see a shadow demon you report it to a Mystical Knight first unless it's attacking you but even then you should use your weapons first to conserve your strength. Do you understand?" Said Dominic.
   "I understand, I am sorry." I said and looked at Liv.
She nodded but she still looked mad.

"Right, I will stay here with Liv a bit longer so she can rest, all of you can run back to the tower and get something to eat, but Rose I want you to report to Odin's office first and tell him what happened here." Said Dominic.

I nodded and followed the others back, but I kept glancing all around me as I jogged, as I knew I was right, there had been a shadow demon, and I could still sense one nearby. I wondered why the others didn't see it and why the shapeshifters didn't sense it with their instincts.
We all made it back to the gate without trouble and the other students walked off towards the tower, but I hesitated so I could take some deep breaths of air to help calm me down and to make sure we

weren't being followed, I also took my jacket off as the sun had come out from behind the clouds and it was starting to warm up. I noticed Iris was walking back towards me.

"Are you alright Rose?" She asked.
  "Yes, I am sorry about before, I hope I didn't scare you." I replied.
  "No, it's fine, accidents happen, we all make mistakes. I'm sure the others will forgive you soon so don't worry."
  "Thank you." I said.

She nodded and walked back towards the tower, once I was sure the jewel had cooled down, I followed her but instead of going to the cafeteria I headed to Odin's office.
I got to his door and stopped. Odin was already mad at me I didn't want to go in, but I knew Dominic would ask him if I had been and he might have even told him I was coming on his S.C.D. So, I took another deep breath and knocked on the door.

"Come in." Shouted Odin.
I opened the door and walked in, Odin was stacking books up on his bookshelf, he glanced at me, and I gave him a nervous smile.

He sighed and said, "Take a seat Rose."

I sat down, put my jacket on my knees and tried to think of an easy way to explain what happened without getting myself into more trouble.

"So, Dominic told me what happened, are you

alright?" He asked as he sat down in his chair
opposite me.

Well, I guess I can't leave anything out, I glanced
down at the jewel.
   "I'm fine, I didn't mean to aim my magic at Liv I
just thought I saw a shadow demon and I guess I
overreacted, sorry." I explained.
   "I understand Rose, it's alright but from now on
try not to use your magic unless you are in a
magic lesson, or you feel like you have no other
choice. I already have the Mystic Council asking
questions about your magic, I don't want to give
them any reason to stop you from becoming a
Mystical Knight."

"OK." I nodded and looked back down at the jewel
it was glowing a light blue again which usually
happened when I was nervous or worried about
something.

"Rose if anything else is bothering you, remember
you can always talk to me about it, and I will help
the best I can." Said Odin.
   "I know it's just...." Before I could finish, there
was a knock at the door.

"Ah, I have a meeting now, but you know where to
find me if you need to talk, you can come back
later if you want and try not to cause any more
trouble, alright?" Smiled Odin.
   "Yes sir." I said and smiled back.

Odin got up from his chair and opened the door
and three men wearing orange robes walked in,
they were from the Mystic Council. All three looked

at me and frowned, Tristan followed them in, and he looked annoyed but smiled when he saw me.
I got up from my chair and walked over to Odin at the door.

"Go and get some rest Rose and make sure you get some food too; you don't want to be hungry at your next lesson." Said Odin as he held the door open for me.

I smiled, nodded, and walked out of the door but before the door closed behind me, I heard a voice in my head.
   "**Are you alright Rose**?" Asked Tristan.

I glanced behind me and saw Tristan holding the door open.

I smiled, "**Yes.**" I lied and quickly walked off before he could stop me.

I heard the door close behind me and I headed back to my room.

Chapter 7.
Fairy Law.

I was stood on my balcony eating the last of my apple and studying the map of my new home. My next lesson will start soon in classroom three on the third floor, I had already changed into my student uniform, and it fit great.

I had decided against going to the cafeteria with the other students for breakfast, and luckily I had my flask of water and a spare apple in my bag. I didn't want to see the others looking at me with fear and I didn't want to talk to anyone about what happened, I had a feeling everyone would know about the incident by now. Also, I had wanted to get some more sleep but sadly that had not happened, so I was still tired.

A white dove flew down from the sky and landed next to me, it started pecking at the balcony looking for food. I put my apple core down next to it and smiled as I watched it eat. I wish I could make friends with the other students as fast as I can with animals, then maybe I wouldn't feel so lonely, I know one group of Mystical Knights cares for me, but as they are busy with other things I haven't been able to see them as much as I would like.

I sighed and went back into my room and grabbed the books I needed before heading out into the corridor.

The corridor was quiet as nearly everyone was in other rooms working or outside and I could also sense some were still eating in the cafeteria. I headed towards the stairs but stopped and turned around as I suddenly sensed someone behind me, and I wasn't happy with who it was.

"What are you doing here?" I asked him.

His dark blue eyes lit up and he pulled his hood down from his head and rubbed his short black hair, then he waved his arm at me. His hand had burnt away on the day he died, by my magic.
  "So, you are no longer ignoring me now." Said Caleb.

I have been seeing Caleb's ghost for a while now, he first appeared to me at Greenfield Village once the magic repel was off my arm. He usually just blames me for his death and then tries to get me to join the Dark Shadow Guild so I decided to ignore him and hoped he would leave; I hadn't seen him since moving here so I had hoped my plan had worked, but I guess I was wrong.

"I didn't think I would see you here." I said.
  "Where you go, I go. We are connected now, that's what happens when you kill someone. It haunts you forever." He said and smiled.
  "Really, how many times do I have to apologize? You know it was an accident, you should go and rest in peace." I said.
  "Haunting you is more fun though and I know you will miss me if I leave."
  "Just go away, your making me late for my lesson." I said and turned back around to leave.

"Do you really believe these knights can teach you how to control your magic, when they only look at you with fear and hatred. You will understand soon where you truly belong." He said.

I turned around to yell at him, but he had vanished.

I took a deep breath and walked down the stairs, I was glad no one else was about. If anyone saw me talking to myself and realize I was talking to ghosts I didn't know what would happen and it was my fault Caleb was dead, so I didn't want the others to worry.

I hurried down the stairs as I realized I was going to be late for my next lesson and that was not a good start to becoming a Mystical Knight.

I got to the classroom without further delay and pushed open the door, the other students were already sat at their desks and the teacher frowned at me as I walked in. She was stood near a black board at the front of the class and her silver eyes lit up as she watched me.

"So, you must be the new student, please take a seat Rose, you are late." She said as she tucked a strand of her dark brown hair behind her ears.

"I'm sorry." I said and sat down in an empty chair closest to me.

The fairy walked over to my desk and smiled, "Do not worry, just try to be on time next lesson. My name is Ebony Blossom, welcome to your lesson of fairy law."

"Thank you." I said and smiled; I should have known a fairy would be teaching this lesson.

Ebony walked back to the front of the class and started talking all about the history of fairies and

how to act around them, especially around the royal family. As a Mystical Knight you may have to do important jobs for them so it's important to understand the way they live.
I tried to concentrate on the lesson, but I kept thinking about what Caleb had said and hearing Liv telling Joseph being around me was dangerous also didn't help. She obviously hadn't forgiven me yet, I tried to ignore them and continued jotting down notes about what Ebony was telling us about fairies.

As the lesson finished Ebony handed me a book and said, "This book will explain all about the law and culture of fairies, it is yours to keep so try to study it the best you can."

I took the book and nodded then Ebony turned to the other students and said, "Please read chapter three on the different magic fairies can use, as there will be a test next lesson and we will discuss it more in detail then too."

"OK." Everyone said.
  "Good. Now remember; today you can all go to the city and have some fun but remember to stick together and be safe." Said Ebony and smiled as the other students hurried out the room talking excitedly.

Before I could follow them Ebony stopped me and said, "Rose if you feel like you need more help or have any more questions about fairies please let me know and I will help you whenever you need it."
  "Ok thank you." I said.

"I should be the one thanking you, you did help our princess. Thank you." She said and bowed her head.

"Ah, it was nothing, they are my friends so I will always help them, and they do more for me anyway." I replied shyly.

"Well off you go and have some fun with your friends." She smiled and held the door open for me.

I nodded and left the room.

I headed back to my room and changed out of my uniform and made sure I brought my thinner jacket. The day was warm, but I wasn't sure how long I would be out for, and it might get cooler later on again, I grabbed my bag, and I also tucked my dagger into my belt hopefully I wouldn't need it. I left the tower and headed towards the gate with the path that would take me to the city, I noticed the other students in there groups walking down the path on the other side of the gate, they were leaving without me. I sighed out loud and wondered if I should still go.

"What is wrong Rose?" Asked Lucas who had suddenly appeared beside me.

"Hi Lucas, the other students left without me. I guess I'm too scary to go with them to the city." I replied.

"Don't be silly, the others probably just got too excited and forgot to wait for you. I know, why don't I go with you, I know all the best places." Said Lucas.

"Alright, thanks. Lets go." I laughed and skipped towards the gate.

Lucas laughed too and followed me, I gave my name to the guard, and he nodded and waved me through, I had to stop myself from giving him Lucas's name too, that would have been difficult to explain.

I walked down the long widening path to the city with Lucas floating beside me, I could already hear all the sounds. Music playing, talking, and laughing and the merchants shouting about the goods they were selling.
Once we got to the city the first thing my eyes focused on was the huge stone cathedral in front of me, its large stained-glass windows were sparkling in the sun and two stone lions with their mouths open as they roared were standing guard at the door.

"Wow." I said.
   "Yes I knew you would like that; it is called Sunshine Cathedral, and it has been there for hundreds of years." Explained Lucas.

I nodded and looked around me, all the buildings had the same light brown color and grey roofs, but they had different decorations and flowers around them, the streets of the city looked old but also looked well looked after, the cobbled paths looked clean, and they were a lot of colorful plants scattered around to brighten the place up.
Everyone looked happy to be there.

I decided to have a look around the market, the food looked and smelled great, and I ended up buying a bag of cookies, they were yummy, and I had to stop myself from offering one to Lucas as

during the excitement I had forgotten he was a
ghost.
   "Don't eat them too fast." He laughed.

We continued to walk around the city, and we
looked at all the sights, it was wonderful how
magical the place was, it was nothing like
Greenfield Village, you didn't have to hide your
magic; in fact, it was against the law to hide strong
magical items like mine while you were in the city,
you always had to have it on display so you
wouldn't be seen as a threat, though just being
near the jewel of darkness felt like a threat to
most, and I did see many look my way and then
try to avoid me, but I just ignored them.

There were fairies and humans dancing on the
street together, different types of animals running
and playing, and most were shapeshifters and
there were even magicians doing magic for the
children though Lucas explained these were tricks
that anyone can learn and not real magic.

Some of the shops were also selling magical items
like the light stones that help power the lights and
the stone lenses. They even had magical charms
to bring you luck, though Lucas claims these are
just for fun, and they don't work. There was also a
shop near the blacksmiths selling weapons, armor,
and riding equipment for horses. And a bookshop
where I ended up buying two books, one about the
history of Sunlight City and one about the legends
of dragons.
I was starting to get tired, but I didn't want to go
back just yet, Lucas saw me yawn.

"If you want to have a rest there is a great place further down the street from here and the food is great too. It's called Brightside Cafe. Nearly all the Mystical Knights like to go there." He said.

"Ok, let's go."

We got further down the street but before we could get to the cafe there was a commotion on the street, people were shouting, and some screamed as they looked up. I followed their gaze up a tall building that looked like it used to be another bell tower, but it had been redesigned into living quarters. And hanging off the roof of the building was a small boy.

"Please someone help him." Shouted a woman.

"We can't get onto the roof, it's too unstable. Any extra weight will make it collapse." Shouted a man from the door.

"Damn it, what are we going to do?" Yelled another man in the crowd.

"HELP!" Screamed the boy.

"Hang on boy!" Shouted an old man beside me.

"This doesn't look good." Said Lucas.

There must be something we can do; is there a magic I can use. I tried to think of something I had read in the jewel of darkness book that could help but I couldn't, and it was too late. The boy fell.

Chapter 8.
Falling Down.

I lifted my arm up and pointed towards the boy, the jewel of darkness lit up a bright green and a magic shield wrapped around the boy, and he floated towards the ground. The crowd gasped and everyone turned towards me and stared.

The magic shield disappeared, and I fell to my knees as using too much magic had affected my body and I had never used that spell before.

"Jason, are you alright?" Shouted a tall woman with dark brown hair and orange eyes, she was a wolf shapeshifter. She ran to the boy and hugged him.
  "Sorry mother." Cried Jason.

Some of the crowd laughed, everyone was happy the boy was now safe. I smiled but was struggling to catch my breath and the jewel was starting to glow a deep blue instead.
  "**Rose?**" Said Lucas beside me, he looked worried, and he was fading.

"You did this with your magic?" Asked the old man who was beside me.
  I looked up and noticed everyone was watching me again, so I took a deep breath and slowly got to my feet. As I did, the jewel sparked with yellow light as it wanted to use more magic.
  "Wait is that the jewel of darkness?" Shouted another woman in the crowd.

Everyone gasped and some even moved away from me, even after saving a boy people were scared of me. I heard someone saying I was a curse, and I felt the jewel heat up as it sensed my anger and worry.
I started to back away from the crowd but then I bumped into someone behind me, I spun around.
   "I'm sorry…." I started to apologize but a familiar face was smiling at me.
   "Well done Rose, thank you for saving Jason." Said Tristan in a loud voice so everyone could hear.
   "That was great." said Clover beside him.
Jaxon and Gray, who were with them bowed at me and they both looked happy.

"It's the prince." A woman shouted.
   And all the crowd bowed towards him, I was about to do the same, but he put his hand on my arm and shook his head.

The boy's mother suddenly ran up to us and gave me a hug.
"Thank you miss for saving my boy, myself and the pack will help you whenever you need it." She said.
   "Um…. It's Ok." I replied.
"Yeah, well done miss." Said the old man beside me.
   "That was great magic." Shouted another boy.

More people gathered around to say thanks and to compliment me, I blushed and laughed as I didn't know what to say. The boy I saved finally came over to me, he had been with his father who hadn't been happy with him for being reckless.

"Thank you for saving me." He said and bowed.

"It's alright, just stay on the ground in the future." I replied.

"She is right Jason; wolves are not meant to climb on roofs." Said Tristan.

"I know, sorry, we were playing hide and seek to practice tracking so I thought I would hide up there but as I was looking over the edge the roof collapsed." Explained Jason.

"I see, we will have to get this checked." Said Tristan and he looked at Gray, he nodded, took a notepad out of his pocket and he jotted something down.

"So, Rose how did you do that?" Asked Clover as the crowd started to move away.

"I don't know, I have never used that spell before. I guess the jewel sensed my need to want to save the boy and it reacted." I replied.

"Are you feeling alright? We saw you collapse after you used your magic." Said Tristan and he looked concerned.

"Yes, I'm alright just tired. I was heading to a place called Brightside Cafe, I heard it was a great place to have a rest and now I need it." I smiled.

"Yes it is our favorite place, I will come with you." Said Clover.

"You don't have to if you're busy."
"Don't be silly Rose, I'm coming. I want to have fun with my friend, and we were going there soon anyway, right Tristan?"

"Yeah we were, but I'm afraid I will have to leave now. I will have to have a look at this building and check up on some of the wolf pack." Sighed Tristan.

"I guess it's not all fun and games being a prince."
I said and smiled.

"You have no idea. Just make sure you two have
fun and stay safe." Said Tristan and he walked off
with his guards.

"Don't worry, we will bring you home some
cakes." Shouted Clover.
Tristan turned back around and waved at us
before he walked into the building.

"Come on Rose it's this way." Said Clover as she
linked arms with mine and we walked off down the
path together.

We got to Brightside Café, it is a large old stone
building in the middle of the city, but it has a warm
and inviting feeling to it. There was a lot of people
sitting at the small tables outside the cafe, but we
headed inside.
Inside had a few tables around a large unlit
fireplace, the food smelled delicious, and I heard
my stomach rumble.
Clover led me to another door inside, where a
waiter was stood.

"Ah, welcome back Princess Clover." He said.

"Hello Mark, this is my friend Rose. Can we go
in?" Asked Clover.

"Yes, there isn't a meeting in there today. I hope
you both have a nice meal." Said Mark and he
held the door open for us both.

"Thank you." I said as I entered the room.

This room also had tables and benches set up and
another smaller fireplace, but this room looked
grander with banners and tapestries hanging on

the walls and a large picture of a tiger above the
fireplace which I assumed was the shapeshifter
king. A couple of Mystical Knights were sat at one
of the tables eating a large meal and as we
entered they stood up and bowed. Clover waved
at them, and they sat down to continue eating. We
walked to another table that was empty and sat
down.

"This room is reserved for Mystical Knights and
the royal families, sometimes they have meetings
here though, so we have to make sure before we
enter. Even the shapeshifter king has come here
for dinner, but he hasn't been here for a while."
Explained Clover.
   "Is that him in the picture?" I asked as Clover
handed me a menu off the table.
   "Yes, though he looks bigger up close." She
replied and smiled as she saw my eyes grow wide.

The drawing was well done, and the tiger was
huge in the picture so I wasn't sure if I wanted to
meet him if he were bigger than that, the tiger's
orange eyes looked like they were watching us,
and you knew if you got him angry you would be in
trouble.

I glanced down at the menu, but I wasn't sure
what to get, even though I was hungry I didn't
fancy a big meal yet after using my magic. A hand
pointed down at the menu.
   **"If I were you, I would get some cheese
scones and some milk, that always made me
feel better after using my magic."** Said Lucas,
who had appeared beside me, and he looked
clearer again.

I was worried when I had seen him vanish in the crowd outside.

"Have you decided what you want?" Asked Clover.
"Yes, have you?" I asked her.
"Yes, I think I will get some pasta." She replied as she waved at a waitress nearby.
"Hello Princess Clover, I see you have brought a new friend. What would you like today?" Asked the waitress who had walked over to the table.
"Hello Maria, this is Rose. Please can I have the pasta special today with some orange juice and a box of cakes to take back to Prince Tristan." Replied Clover.
"Of course, and what would you like Rose?" Asked Maria as she looked at me.
"Can I have two cheese scones and a glass of milk please." I said.
"Alright, I will be back soon." She said and walked out of the room through another door in the back.

Clover was looking at me with a weird look on her face.
"What's wrong?" I asked.
"Oh nothing, it's just you have ordered the same thing Lucas and Tristan used to order. It was Lucas's favorite thing to order especially when he had used his magic, he always said it made him feel better. And I have not seen Tristan order it since he died." Clover said sadly.
"Oh right, I guess we have the same taste in food then." I said and glanced at Lucas who looked sad beside me.
"Yeah, well there are nice scones." Smiled Clover.

After a short wait Maria came back with our order of food, drinks, and the box of cakes.

"Here you are, please let me know if you would like anything else." She said as she placed them on the table.

"Thank you." We both said at the same time and laughed.

Maria smiled then walked to the other table as the other Mystical Knights wanted her.
While we ate Clover asked. "So, Rose what do you think of Sunlight City?"

"It's great, I didn't realize how big and magical the place would be, it's definitely different than Greenfield Village." I replied.

"Yes, the city is busier than what you're used to but I'm sure you will get used to it, how are you getting on with the other students?"

"Um…well. I don't think they like me much." I replied.

"What! Who wouldn't like someone like you, you are a really nice person." She said as she slammed her cup down in madness.

"Thank you Clover, you are really nice too, but it's complicated. I guess I didn't make a great first impression." I laughed.

"Oh yeah, but that was an accident they shouldn't stay mad at you for that, anyway I heard Edmund was even worse when he was a student." Smiled Clover.

"Wait, you heard about what happened?" I asked.

"Everyone knows, you can't keep secrets in that tower, but don't worry I'm sure they will want to be friends with you."

"Yeah maybe." I sighed and drank the last of my milk.

We suddenly heard the bells chime on the clock tower.
"Wow is that the time already. I better get back or Marigold will wonder where I am, will you be heading back home now?" Asked Clover as she stood up to leave.
   "Yes I think I've explored enough for one day." I said and smiled. I got some money out of my pocket ready to pay for my meal.
   "No Rose, this was my treat. A welcome to Sunlight City meal." Said Clover.
   "Are you sure, I can…." Clover gave me an angry look.
   "Ok thank you, it was great." I laughed.

Clover smiled and nodded as she got her money out of her small bag and handed it to Maria. We said thank you and goodbye to the staff and then we headed back outside.

The air was a lot cooler now and it felt like it was about to rain, I wished I had drank some hot tea instead of milk, but Lucas was right it had somehow made me feel better. We both walked back through the city to get to the path to take us home, the city had become quieter now as the shops closed for the night and people went home. As we rounded another corner drops of rain started to fall from the sky.

"Looks like we aren't going to make it home before the rain comes after all." Said Clover.

I nodded and looked in front of us as I heard voices and someone laughing, it was the other students also on the way back home. The rain started to fall heavier, and I could hear Liv complaining her new clothes would get wet, they started to walk faster, but I suddenly stopped as something didn't feel right.

"Rose, what's wrong?" Asked Clover.
  "Something is coming." I replied and looked around me.

Someone screamed in front of us.
The other students were in trouble, my eyes zoomed in, and I could see shadow demons in the form of men holding swords all around them.

We both ran to help them, luckily my injured arm was not the one I used to hold my dagger, the shadows were everywhere, and the other students fought them off with their daggers, a wolf and a bear appeared beside us as Jasper and T.J. changed form.

"We have to get back to the tower!" Shouted Yara.
  "Where did these things come from." Yelled Liv.

I used my dagger on another shadow I wanted to use my magic, but I hesitated as I knew I hadn't fully recovered yet. Luckily, the others were good fighters too, so we held them off well, but the shadows had more numbers, and more were coming. I also noticed the shadows weren't aiming their attacks at me; they were focusing on the others, and I didn't know why.

"Come on, we need to move." I shouted and started running down the street towards the castle grounds.

The others followed me, and the shadows gave chase, we managed to get to the path but then we suddenly had to stop as we heard drumming and more shadows, in wolf form this time, appeared in front of us. We automatically gathered in a circle to defend each other.

"Woah!" Shouted Clover as she dodged an attack.
  "Are you alright Clover?" I shouted as I took out another demon that I got in front of as it was trying to attack Clover too, it managed to cut my face before it vanished.
  "Yes." She huffed beside me.
"We need help, has anyone got an S.C.D. with them?" Shouted Joseph.

No one said yes and I had left mine in my room.
  "Clover, fly to the tower for help. We will hold them off." I yelled.
  "I can't leave you." She replied.
"It's fine, we can't fight like this forever. Now go." I said as I saw more coming behind us.

"I will go too; you also need protection princess." Said Iris.

Both fairies dropped their bags and turned small in a flash of white light and flew fast towards the tower, and I tried to contact Tristan, hopefully he would be close enough to hear me.

"Tristan if you can hear me, Clover is flying back home.

Sunlight City, A Mystical Knight Novel book 2.
By Jade Stephenson ©.

We need help on the path towards the city, shadow...."

Before I could finish a shadow pounced on Yara beside me and I lost my concentration. I used some magic to destroy it and then I blasted a few more nearby but somehow that only made things worse as more appeared in front of us.

"Rose! What did you do?" Yelled Liv.

"It wasn't me!" I shouted back, though I wasn't sure.

We all kept fighting as the rain fell but it was making the ground slippery and a few times my feet had slipped, and Liv had fell to the ground but luckily Joseph had managed to pick her back up again and I could tell the others were getting tired too.

I was worried we weren't going to last much longer but then I heard a roar, and I smiled, Tristan had joined the fight followed by a pack of wolves, Edmund, and a few Kings Guards on horses. I knew then we would be alright.

As the last of the shadow demons were defeated, we stopped to catch our breaths and the Kings Guards checked the other student's injuries, but I stayed back and made my eyes zoom in around the area to make sure no more shadows were about.

"You can stand down now Rose, it's clear." Said Tristan who had changed back into his human form and had come up beside me.

I still had a strong grip on my dagger, and I was still on edge, I had also heard Liv telling one of the guards that as soon as I had used my magic more demons had appeared, and it was a curse to be near me.

"Rose are you alright?" Asked Tristan as he held his hand out and touched my cheek where the demon had scratched my face.
 I nodded and put my dagger back inside its sheath on my belt.
 "Are Clover and Iris alright? They both flew back to the tower." I asked.

"They are both fine, we made them wait back there." Said Edmund who had heard my question.
 "I heard your call and then we spotted the fairies as we were getting ready to leave, Clover quickly told us what had happened. I'm glad everyone is alright." Said Tristan.
 "Thanks to you." I smiled.

"Alright everyone lets head back to the tower. You all did a great job defending each other, well done." Shouted Dominic, who had also come and had changed back into his human form so he could communicate with us better.

We all walked back to the tower slowly and in silence, the Kings Guards and wolves stayed beside us on alert to make sure we got back without any more trouble. A few of us had injuries but they didn't look too serious, Liv had hurt her ankle, so she was getting a lift back on one of the horses. I only had the cut on my cheek but it wasn't too deep so I knew it would heal in a few

hours.
What worried me more was the fact the demons had been attacking the others and were ignoring me and now the other students were looking at me with fear in their eyes.

Chapter 9.
Meeting Layla.

I was in the forest again; I had woken up too early
and couldn't get back to sleep so I had decided to
go for a walk with Silver. I climbed onto his bare
back and gently held onto his mane. I was glad my
arm felt a lot better today, I didn't need to put his
tack on as I only use that now when we go on
longer journeys or when we compete in shows.
The Kings Guard at the gate wasn't happy about
letting me out alone and so early in the morning
but he waved me through the gate and told me to
be careful.

However right now I was surrounded by shadow
demons, I slowly dismounted Silver and pulled out
the sword from my belt. They didn't attack, they
stood still and stared at me with their blood red
eyes. Silver banged his left hoof to the ground and
huffed, then a figure walked out of the darkness, it
was Caleb.

"The Mystical Knights don't trust you Rose, so why
do you stay with them?" He said.
  "Do you trust me?" I asked.
"Yes, I do." He smiled.
  "Did you forget who killed you, I'm the last person
you should trust." I laughed.
  "If you come with me now and join my guild, all
will be forgiven." He replied.

"No." I said, but I had hesitated, and I could tell by
the look on Caleb's face he had realized that too.

"Alright I will wait but members from the Shadow Guild have joined the Mystical Knights, so it's only fair someone comes over to our side." He said and smiled.

"What?"

The shadow demons started to disappear and then Caleb started to walk away.

"Wait…. What do you mean? Caleb!" I shouted. It was too late he had gone and so had all the shadow demons.

The jewel of darkness heated up and turned a dark blue as it sensed my frustration and worry, Silver rubbed his head against my arm, and I sighed out loud and gave him a pat on the neck.

"Don't worry, lets head back now." I said and he bent his head down so I could climb back onto his back.

We got back to the gate without any more unexpected guests appearing and the guard waved us back through, I dismounted Silver and decided to head back to the fields with him as it was still too early for my lesson, and I didn't want any breakfast yet. As we walked, some wolves stopped in front of us and bowed their heads at me and I wondered if they had heard about me saving Jason, I smiled and waved at them and continued to the stables. Leah saw us coming.

"Hi Rose, you're up early did you go for a ride?" She asked.

"Morning Leah, yes we went out to the forest I'm just going to put Silver back in the fields now, but can I grab a brush? I would like to give him a groom too."

"Yes that's fine, the brushes are in that end stable with the other supplies, your bag is there too" She replied.

"Thank you." I said and went inside the stable while Silver waited for me outside.

This stable was used as a tack room and inside was all the grooming, medical, riding equipment and rugs for all the horses that lived here but it also had spare supplies for the horses of anyone visiting the tower or castle. It was a lot bigger then the room we used at Unicorn Stables, luckily I found the small bag I had brought with me. Inside was Silver's grooming supplies, Willow had given some of the brushes to me as a gift when I first started looking after Silver. I grabbed a hard brush and headed back outside, then I followed Silver to the fields.

I opened the nearest gate and Silver trotted through, then he bent his head down and started munching the grass, while he ate I started to brush his soft black hair on his back. I glanced up and noticed some of the other horses had moved closer to us, but I noticed they still kept their distance from Silver as they probably sensed he was not to be messed with and he was bigger than the others. As I brushed Silver I watched Ethan catch another horse in the field for a Mystical Knight who was waiting nearby, and my mind started to think about the words Caleb spoke, and I wondered if he was telling the truth, was someone really here from the Dark Shadow Guild?

"What's on your mind Rose?" Asked Lucas as

he appeared beside me.

"Oh, hello Lucas, I'm just thinking about something Caleb said to me." I replied.

"Caleb?"

"Um, yes in a dream I had. He said members from the Dark Shadow Guild had joined the Mystical Knights." I said.

I had forgotten I hadn't told him I also see Caleb's ghost and I decided I still didn't want to tell anyone about it yet.

"I'm sure it's nothing to worry about it is just a bad dream, Caleb has gone now and I'm sure the Mystical Knights would know if something like that had happened." Explained Lucas as he patted Silver on the neck and even though he was a ghost somehow Silver knew he was there, he looked up at him and then continued to eat the grass.

"Yeah, you're probably right." I sighed but I still had a bad feeling and the fact that shadow demons were appearing again couldn't be a coincidence.

"If you're really worried about it maybe you should talk to Odin about it."

"No, it's alright, I don't want him to worry. He has a lot on his mind already."

"Well alright but don't you worry too much about it too, you know it affects your magic, and you should really talk to someone who isn't a ghost about your problems." Smiled Lucas.

"But then I would miss your great advice." I laughed.

"Well yes you're right about that." Laughed Lucas.

I smiled and looked up at the sky it was starting to get lighter, and I felt hungry.
   "I better go and get some breakfast before my magic history lesson, see you both later." I said and patted Silver on the neck.
   "Ok, bye Rose." Said Lucas and Silver neighed.

I walked back out of the field, put my brush back in the tack room and waved at Ethan and Leah who I spotted tacking up another horse, then I headed back to the tower.
After a wash I changed into my student uniform and went to the cafeteria. As it was still early few people were about, but I could hear more sounds coming from upstairs as they woke up and started getting ready for the day.

They were a couple of shapeshifters sat around a large table having breakfast and I could also see Tristan was with them, Gray was next to him, and he was reading something while the others listened carefully as they ate. I decided not to disturb them as I didn't want to get into trouble and I decided to grab a bowl of porridge and a cup of tea and went to sit in the indoor garden instead, and while I ate I studied the maps of the tower and grounds. I realized the grounds were a lot bigger than I thought, I hadn't even been around half, and I had not seen the cottages where some of the shapeshifters lived with their families, I had heard Tristan's and Lucas's parents also lived there. I would need to explore more especially if this were going to be my home from now on.

After a while I noticed it was time for my Magic History lesson and I didn't want to be late, Odin was teaching us, and I was looking forward to it. I folded up my maps, took my empty bowl and cup back to the kitchen then headed back upstairs.
The lesson was on the third floor in classroom four. I got to the door, and I could hear voices, I put my hand on the handle took a deep breath and walked inside.
The other students were sat at their desks talking but as they noticed me they stopped, I quickly sat down in an empty seat at the back of the room and sighed.

"Hey Rose, what's it like to be a hero?" Asked Jasper.
 I looked at him surprised; he sounded friendly.
"Yeah Rose that catch was great, I bet little Jason was terrified. We are glad you saved him." Said T.J.
 "Yeah, me too, thanks." I replied and smiled back at them.
 "How did you do it?" Asked Iris.
"Um, I don't really know, it just happened." I replied.
 "Wow." Said Liv sarcastically.

Before anyone else could say something, Odin walked into the room.
"Good morning students." He said.
 "Good morning." We all replied.

He smiled and walked to his desk but before he got started with the lesson he looked my way and nodded, and I waved and smiled back.

Sunlight City, A Mystical Knight Novel book 2.
By Jade Stephenson ©.

"Good everyone is here, today we will be reading up on the history of Fairy magic and how they use it today, and also about the time they started to help the humans, as we have a fairy in the class you can ask her about anything you don't understand, and I will help too." Odin explained as he took a book out of his desk draw.

"Please turn to page eleven in your book and remember to take notes as we read, as you may need to go back to this topic in the future." He said, then he walked over to my desk and handed me the book.

"This book is yours to keep Rose, it will help you understand a lot more about magic history and the magic different species use. If you want to know more, please ask me and I will help you the best I can." Smiled Odin.
   "Thank you Odin." I replied and opened the book to the first page.

I noticed there was a message inside, it read 'Dear Rose, I hope you do well in your studies and become an official Mystical Knight soon, best of luck from Robert Odin.'

I looked back up at him and smiled, he winked and walked back to the front of the class.
I turned to page eleven and Odin started to read his book out loud, as we read ours, and I made notes in my note book of some of the important parts I may need to remember later on, Odin also stopped reading some parts to explain more in detail and with the help of Iris we all learnt a lot about the history of Fairies.

The lesson was interesting, and it helped distract me from my thoughts on Caleb and the Dark Shadow Guild.

"Right, that is all for today. I want you all to complete a report on the different magic fairies can use and how they use it has changed throughout the years, use your books and I will allow you to ask a fairy for help if you need it. You can all hand it to me next lesson. Dismissed." Said Odin.

The other students got up to leave but before they could, a wolf pushed open the door and walked in. The students backed away and looked scared and even Jasper who is also a wolf avoided eye contact and quickly left the room and the others followed, only Odin looked happy to see the wolf.

"Hello Layla, I hope you have been staying out of trouble today." He said and he bent down and patted the wolf on the head.
I got up and walked over to them.
"Ah, Rose this is my daughter Layla, Layla this is Rose." Said Odin.

Layla walked up to me, and I held my hand out towards her nose so she could learn my scent and I had learnt this was the best way to greet a shapeshifter so they wouldn't feel threatened, and you could gain their trust. Layla rubbed her head against my hand, and she seemed happy. I smiled and looked up at Odin, but he looked shocked.

"What's wrong?" I asked.
"Oh nothing, it's just normally Layla stays away from other humans or acts aggressively towards

them. I am glad she seems to like you." He smiled.
Layla sat down beside me and looked up at her
father.
Her mother was a wolf shapeshifter but when she
sadly passed away, Layla changed into her wolf
form and has never changed back into her human
form since. Isabella had told me when
shapeshifters suffer loss and grieve sometimes
they would stay in animal form for a while to help
cope, but Layla has stayed this way even longer
than most and no one knows if she will ever
change back. I know how she feels, losing your
mother hurts.

"Well, I hope we can become good friends, would
that be alright Layla?" I asked.
   As I bent down Layla moved closer to me and
rubbed her head against my head then licked my
cheek, I laughed and gently stroked her head.
   "That means yes, I'm glad." Laughed Odin then
he suddenly pulled us both into a hug and said, "I
hope both of you will be alright."

"Um…. Thank you Odin, but I am alright." I replied
and Layla whimpered and licked his face.
   Odin sighed, got back up then looked at us both
and said "Remember I can tell when something is
bothering you two, I know I'm not your real father
Rose, but I've come to think of you as my own
daughter just like Layla. If both of you need any
help you know you can come to me, alright?"
   I nodded and smiled, "You don't have to worry
I'm fine."
I decided not to tell him, as I knew he had enough
on his mind with helping Tristan look after Sunlight
City while the king was away.

"Rose you look exhausted, there must be something wrong, and your eye is still red." Odin said.

"It is nothing really, I think I'm just finding it harder to settle into my new home. And I don't know why my eye is still red, maybe it is something to do with using stronger magic, sorry I know you told me not to, but there was a boy in the city and…"
    "No! Don't apologize for saving someone's life, I heard all about it and I'm proud of you. I just want you to stay safe and be happy. I'm sure you will settle in soon, just let me know if you need anything and I will help." Said Odin.

"Thank you Odin but you help me enough already." I replied.
    "Well anyway still let me know and I would like you to go to Doctor Wesley and let him check your eyes to be safe."
    "Ok I will, well I better go, I wanted to explore more around the grounds before my next lesson. If this is my home now I would like to be able to find my way around without a map." I laughed.
    "Well alright, yes that is a good idea just stay safe." Said Odin.
    "I will be fine." I smiled and opened the door to leave but I noticed Layla was following me.

"Do you want to come with me Layla? I asked.
    Layla rubbed her head against my leg and left the room, then she stopped and looked back at me. I guess she wants me to follow her.
    "Looks like you are getting a guide to show you around." Odin smiled.

I laughed, waved at Odin then followed Layla back
down the stairs and out the front door.

I noticed a few Mystical Knights and Kings Guards
were glancing our way and they seemed to want
to avoid us, I wasn't sure if it was because of me
or Layla.
We ended up at the gate that led to the path in the
forest and Layla ran through, the guard looked at
me and nodded so I followed her, he must have
remembered my name as I saw him write it down.
I followed Layla through the trees and smiled,
going for walks, and being surrounded by nature
always made me feel better and listening to all the
different birds singing calmed me down. I suddenly
heard wolves howling and then I saw them running
through the trees to my right, Layla took off after
them and it looked like they were friends. I guess I
will be exploring alone now but I didn't mind.

I looked down at the map I had pulled from my
pouch, the forest was huge but only a small part of
it was used for training and another part behind
the castle was private for the king. I decided to
walk up to the end point on the map, so I knew
where the path stopped, in case I needed to know
in the future, I noticed it was just passed the check
point where we had run to during training.
As I walked I tried to take in my surroundings so I
would remember the way without the map. My
eyes focused on the different types of plants and
trees around me, and my ears also picked up the
different sounds, I heard the wolves howling again
in the distance and I sensed something running
towards me on my right. I stopped and waited, and
three large boars ran out of the bushes, luckily

they ran past me and headed off, I guess the
wolves spooked them. I had to be more careful in
this forest as it was home to a lot of different
species of animals, I was normally alright around
animals though, even the predators. My family at
Unicorn Stables always said I had a magic touch
when it came to animals, I could always
understand them even before I got the jewel of
darkness. I wondered if that's why I seem to get
along better with the shapeshifters too. In this
forest though, it wasn't just the animals living here,
Tristan had told me stories before about the other
magical creatures living here so I still had to be
careful as not all of them were friendly.

I made it to the checkpoint we had come to during
training and I noticed the cart we had placed the
bags on had already gone, the other Mystical
Knights must have picked it up and took it to the
mountains. The map showed the boarder to be
just up ahead so I carried on walking but as I got
closer, I felt someone was near me, I turned
around and put my hand on my sword.
Suddenly shadow demons appeared around me,
their evil red eyes gleamed bright in the sun as
they moved closer to attack. I took out my sword
and started to fight back, I didn't want to use my
magic as I feared I would lose control again and it
would weaken me. As the demons came forward,
one at a time I took them out and dodged attacks.

As I took out another demon I heard a wolf howl, I
glanced beside me and saw Layla run out from
behind some trees and pounce on the nearest
demons, I smiled, I was happy I had help now, as I
was getting tired. We fought the last demons off

together and no more appeared, I stood still and breathed in deep, to get my breath back. Layla walked up to me and whimpered.

"Thank you Layla, are you alright?" I asked her.
   She rubbed her head up against my leg and I somehow knew that meant she was fine but was worried about me.
   "I'm alright, let's get back to the tower before any more show up." I said.

We started walking back the way we had come, and I wondered why the shadows had appeared to attack me if the Dark Shadow Guild wanted me to join them and the demons didn't fight as hard as they normally did, they could have all jumped at me together, but they hadn't, and it didn't make sense.
I kept my sword in my hand, and I stayed alert the whole way back, but I definitely felt safer walking beside a wolf.

Before we went through the gate I stopped and said, "Layla, I think I should keep what happened in the forest between us, I don't think I should tell the others yet, it would only worry them, and I want to find out more about the Dark Shadow Guild and why the shadows keep coming. I want to help the others and maybe this is how I can. I have the jewel of darkness for a reason, and I want to find out why, I want to know why it chose me and why I can use the magic inside it."

Layla bent her head down then looked back up at me and I knew she agreed, it helped to talk to someone even if they couldn't talk back.

"Thank you for your help and for listening." I smiled.

Layla walked back through the gate, and I sighed, put my sword back in its sheath and followed her, the guard nodded at us both and we both walked back to the tower together.

Chapter 10.
The Shadows book.

I started walking towards the large greenhouses that were behind Sunrise Tower. This was where my next lesson would be, the Study of Plants and Herbs, and Isabella would be teaching it. I glanced down beside me and smiled, Layla had decided to follow me, she was probably still worried after the attack and wanted to keep an eye on me. I was worried too and annoyed, as because of the shadow demons I was late again for my lesson, and I wondered if that was their plan from the start.

The two large greenhouses were huge, one was used to grow some fruit and vegetables and the other was for plants and herbs and according to the map it was also home to many butterflies. The lesson would take place inside the plant and herb greenhouse, I spotted the sign and pushed open the door and walked into a smaller room that held some garden tools and equipment.
I could hear voices coming from behind the second door that was in front of me, so I opened that door and walked through a curtain that I assumed stopped the butterflies from getting out. Layla walked in beside me and I gasped out loud when I saw the inside, it was like a magical jungle full of different species of plants and herbs, and it smelled wonderful. There was a lot of different colored butterflies flying around us and I could also hear running water coming from somewhere inside.
The greenhouse was warm, so I took off my jacket

and headed towards the voices.

We found the other students sat around two large tables at the far corner of the greenhouse. They looked towards us as we approached.

"You're late Rose." Said Isabella who was stood beside a plant.

"Sorry Isabella, I got lost while exploring the grounds, luckily my friend found me. It won't happen again I promise." I said.

"I see, well take a seat. I'm glad you have joined us too Layla." Replied Isabella, but I could tell by the look on her face she didn't believe me about being lost.

I sat down in an empty seat near Jasper. He smiled at me but looked a little nervous as Layla sat down on the floor beside us.

"Right, Rose do you know what type of plant this is?" Asked Isabella and she pointed at the plant beside her.

I looked at the purple flowers and I recognized them.

"Is it a Prunella Vulgaris plant?" I asked.

"Yes that's right, it is also known as the Heal all plant and the fairies call it the heart of earth, we were just talking about how this plant can help with wounds, I would like you all to think of another plant that also helps heal wounds and draw it in your notebooks and write down all you can about your chosen plant. We will discuss what we found in your next lesson, if you need help you can ask me or the groundskeeper Terran Huckleberry. He should be around here somewhere." Explained Isabella.

A fairy appeared from behind some plants; his silver eyes gleamed as he waved at us then he disappeared again.

The other students got up to walk around the greenhouse to find the right plants, only myself and Joseph stayed behind. Joseph started to draw in his notebook, so I guessed he already knew what plant he wanted to draw. I hesitated as I had heard Liv telling the others that my red eye was the sign of evil and I kept thinking about what Caleb had said and I wondered if one of the students could be part of the Dark Shadow Guild.

Isabella walked back over to the table and asked, "Have you decided what plant you would like to draw?"

I took my mother's notebook out of my pouch and said, "No I haven't decided yet, but would it be alright for me to use this?"

"Yes that is alright, you can use any books if you think it will help you but what book is that? I don't remember seeing it before." Asked Isabella.

"It was my mother's journal; she used to study plants and herbs too and she always made sure when we went for walks around Greenfield Village I knew what types of plants were around me and what they could be used for. I brought this with me hoping it would help during this lesson." I replied.

"I see, that is a good idea I'm sure your mother would be very proud." Smiled Isabella.

"Thank you." I said and smiled back.

"Isabella!" Shouted Liv from the other side of the greenhouse.

Isabella nodded at me then walked over to her.

Once everyone decided we all got to work drawing our plants. I had decided to choose the Lavender plant as it was a plant that my mother loved and it helped ease her illness, it also smells lovely. Drawing helped keep my mind of my worries about the shadow demons, but the lesson was soon over and my thoughts of why the shadow demons had come came back to me. I noticed the other students were leaving the greenhouse and even Layla got up and stretched her legs. I gathered my papers and books up and wondered what I should do with the rest of my day.

"Are you alright Rose?" Asked Isabella.
   "Yes, I'm fine, I was just wondering where I should go to explore next." I replied.
   "Well maybe you should stay close, so you don't get lost again." She laughed.
   "Yes, good plan." I said and laughed too.
"Well, if you need any more books for your other lessons the library would be a good place to start."
   "Good idea, I haven't been there yet." I said and headed to the door where Layla was waiting.

I also thought finding a book about the Dark Shadow Guild or shadow demons may help me understand why they keep coming after me and maybe even a way to stop them.
I opened the door and Layla ran off back in the direction of the forest.
   "Looks like she doesn't want to read." I said and smiled.
   "I'm glad you two have become friends maybe it will help her." Said Isabella.
   "Do you think she will ever become a human again?" I asked.

"Only she knows the answer to that, only time will tell I suppose." She replied.

I nodded, "Well see you later."

Isabella waved at me then went back into the greenhouse.

I headed back to the tower and made my way up to the second floor as I remembered seeing the library, next to Odin's office. I pushed open the door and gasped, the library was huge, there were hundreds of books on large wooden curved bookshelves, and I could also see a small staircase leading up to another part of the library on the floor above. There was a desk near the stairs where a woman was sat talking to two Mystic Council members, I decided not to disturb them and look around the library myself, for the books I wanted.

Further inside there was also some tables for people to sit at to read and do research, a few Mystical Knights and Kings Guards were sat around them, and the room was quiet as they worked. I noticed the books were in alphabetical order and also in categories, all the shelves were labelled so you knew where to look for the books you wanted.

As I walked, I wondered where I would find the books I wanted and would they even have those books in here.

I walked around another bookshelf and ended up in a small space and someone I knew was sat at a small table reading a book.

"Wow, I didn't think I would find you in here." I said and smiled at him when he looked up.

"I have to study too, you know." Tristan replied and laughed.

"Well don't give yourself a headache." I laughed.

Before Tristan could reply, someone else came around the bookshelf, he was a small old man, and he was wearing an orange robe which means he is a member of the Mystic Council. He looked at me and he did not look happy.

"Your Highness, it is time to go back to the castle. I suggest you study there, where there will be less distractions." He said.

"Alright Councilor Vincent, I'm coming." Replied Tristan as he picked up his books.

The councilor then turned to me and said, "And you, young miss, I suggest next time you see him you address the prince in the proper manner to show your respect." Then he walked off.

Tristan followed him but before he left he said through our mind link. **"Don't worry Rose, just keep being yourself."**

"Yeah ok. Good luck prince." I replied and smiled as he waved at me.

"The councilor is right you know, I know your friends with the prince, but it might be best to stay away from him, sometimes being friends with us can cause trouble for royalty." Said Iris who had appeared once Tristan had left.

"Just because he is a prince now, doesn't mean I should stop being his friend." I replied.

"Oh, I know. I didn't mean anything like that, but sometimes we have to make sacrifices for the ones we care for. Being a prince can be difficult he has great responsibilities to protect everyone here and he has to work hard, I'm sure even you wouldn't want to get in the way of that. You have other friends who can help you and you can also ask me, and I will help you the best I can." She said.

"Iris!" Someone shouted from behind another bookcase.
 "Oh, I better go now, I suggest you go check upstairs on bookcase number three if you need any books about the strange creatures that roam around here, see you later." Said Iris and she ran off before I could reply.

I wondered what she meant, did she know what I was looking for and would I really cause trouble for Tristan if I stayed being his friend?
I sighed and decided not to think about that right now and continue my search for the books I wanted.

I decided to head up the stairs to the second part of the library, it was quieter up here as there was only one Kings Guard sat on a chair reading. He looked up at me but didn't say anything, so I continued my search through the bookshelves, I walked to bookcase number three like Iris suggested and I saw the label read, 'History of Dark Magic'.
I read the spines of the books and found a large black book called 'Shadows.' I flicked through the book and knew this was a good place to start, so I decided to take it with me. I headed back down the stairs and went to the desk where the woman was still talking to the Mystic Council members. They

stopped talking when I approached.

"Hello, I would like to borrow this book please." I said and put the book on the desk.

"Hello, of course please tell me your name." She replied as she tucked a strand of her short brown hair behind her ear and got a card out of the desk drawer.

"I'm Rose Ashley." I told her.

"Ah, the new student, it's nice to meet you Rose, I'm Veronica Hope, the librarian. If you need any more books, please let me know." She said and she opened the book but looked confused.

"Strange, I don't recognize this book, and it hasn't got a card inside, maybe it fell out...um maybe it's a new book." Said Veronica, then she got a card from inside a drawer on her desk and wrote down my name, then put it inside the book.

And then she wrote my name down inside a large book on her desk then said, "You have two weeks to read it but if you need any more time, please let me know."

"That is a strange book for a new student to be reading. Are you studying that in one of your lessons?" Said one of the Mystic Council members.

"It is alright Charles, Rose can take any book she wants that is why the library is here, so everyone can learn all they can about the world." Said Veronica and she handed me the book back.

"Thank you." I smiled and left the library before they could ask any more questions.

I headed up the stairs and went back to my room so I could read the book without anyone else seeing. I sat at my desk and opened the book to the first page, it read:

'Shadow demons are dangerous, so stay away from them, they move and act like normal shadows but if you have to fight them any form of weapon will work against them, though magic is more affective. Shadow demons can take on any forms including humans and animals, no one knows where they came from and why they attack anyone nearby, but it is believed they attack to steal the shadows of the people around them to gain more power and become stronger it is also believed they were once involved with dragons. A group called the Dark Shadow Guild has somehow managed to learn how to control the demons and are now using them to steal all magical items. In no way must you try to summon and control shadow demons as this can be fatal.'

Right so nothing really new there, I knew all that except I didn't realize you could try to summon the shadow demons yourself, not that I would try it.
I turned the page and noticed someone else had wrote in the book, it read:

'The Shadow Guild is trying to save the world from the corrupt, we need all magical items to help us, but we mainly need the Jewel of Darkness. The shadow demons can help us too as we control them like the dragon of the past, the Mystical Knights don't understand us and are trying to get in our way, they need to be stopped. This book will help the reader

become one of us, when you are ready you will join
us!'

Wait, did this book belong to someone who was
with the Dark Shadow Guild, I thought. And then I
sensed someone behind me.

"So have you learnt anything new?" Asked Caleb
from behind me and I jumped.
    "Only that the Dark Shadow Guild are idiots, oh
no wait, I already knew that." I replied.
    "Ouch." He said.
"What do you want?" I asked.
    "I was just wondering why you are reading that
book when you can just ask me anything about my
guild and the shadows." He replied.

I turned around and looked at him.
"I didn't think you would tell me anything, I
assumed it was a secret only your guild can
know." I said.
    "Well, we do want you to join our guild
remember, I could let you know some secrets."
Said Caleb.
    "Let me guess, you will only tell me once I agree
to join your guild."
    Caleb nodded but then said, "Well ask me
something, maybe I could tell you something
before you join us."
    "Alright, how exactly do the Dark Shadow Guild
control the shadows and where did they come
from?" I asked.
    "Ah sorry, you can't know that information yet, I
will tell you that, when you join the guild. And I've
told you before stop calling us the Dark Shadow
Guild, it's just Shadow Guild. The Mystical Knights

gave us the dark name."

Before I could ask him something else, he started to walk around the room and then he noticed something on the wall, he was looking at one of Lucas's photos, I looked and saw it was one of Lucas stood next to a young girl.
  "Allena." Said Caleb sadly.

I knew that Allena was the girl Lucas was trying to save, and he was trying to make her leave the Dark Shadow Guild on the day they both died.
  "And if I did join your guild, how do I know I won't just end up like her?" I asked.
  Caleb spun around and shouted.
"The Mystical Knights killed my sister not the Shadow Guild!"

I looked back at the photo shocked; I didn't know Allena was his sister but as I looked closer, I could see the family resemblance they both had the same dark hair and eyes.
  "I'm sorry I didn't know she was your sister." I said and I wondered why Lucas hadn't told me.
  "Something else the Mystical Knights failed to tell you; I wonder what other secrets they are keeping from you." Caleb sighed.

He walked over to the door and then left through a dark portal.

Chapter 11.
A dream about Allena.

I woke up and I was outside, next to the fountain in
Sunlight City. The people around me were a blur
but then I spotted someone I knew, he was clear.
I walked up to him and said, "Lucas, what is
happening, how did I get here?"

"Ah, there you are." He replied but then I noticed
he wasn't looking at me, he was looking past me, I
turned around and saw someone else. It was a
young girl with long dark hair and brown eyes, she
looked about my age and she had a kind face, but
her eyes looked worried. I remembered who she
was, it was Allena the girl Lucas tried to save, and
Caleb's sister.
   She ran up to Lucas and said, "Sorry I'm late, I
thought I was being followed. Are the Mystical
Knights nearby?"

"Yes, don't worry Allena they are hiding in plain
sight, so we are safe to talk." Replied Lucas and
he glanced to his right.
I followed his gaze and spotted Tristan and
Edmund sat together on a bench nearby, they
were talking to each other, but I could tell they
were keeping an eye on Lucas and Allena.
I looked around at the other people around me
and noticed a few more were coming into focus, I
saw Odin, Isabella, Marigold, Clover and even
Jaxon and Gray. I realized now I wasn't awake,
but I wasn't having a normal dream either, I was
somehow seeing a memory from the past.

"I am worried though; I know leaving is for the best but leaving my brother behind doesn't feel right. I don't want him to suffer but he still believes in the Dark Shadow Guild, hopefully he will realize the truth in time." Said Allena.

Before Lucas could reply, something happened, a dark cloud grew around us and I could sense a dark presence, fear grew inside me, and I knew something bad was about to happen.
Suddenly Allena fell to the floor, something had hurt her.

"No!" Yelled Lucas and shadow demons appeared all around us.
  "Allena!" Shouted Caleb as he appeared beside me.

I saw the jewel of darkness glow a dark black around Lucas's neck and electric sparks flashed. Lucas screamed and in a flash of darkness both him and Allena disappeared and only a cloud of black dust was left behind.
  "No, this can't be real, Allena." Whispered Caleb.

"Lucas!" Shouted Tristan and he ran to the spot where only a pile of dust was left, and he fell to his knees.
  "You! This is all your fault, you killed her, the Mystical Knights killed her!" Shouted Caleb and he charged at Tristan's back with his sword drawn.

Tristan didn't move and I was about to call out, forgetting for a moment that this was a memory, luckily Edmund jumped between them and blocked Caleb's attack and more Mystical Knights and Kings Guards appeared. The shadow demons started to vanish and a tall man wearing a dark cloak came and grabbed Caleb by the arm and dragged him through a dark portal. Tristan yelled with all the pain of losing his brother.

The last thing I saw before I woke up was the others gathering around Tristan and I could hear someone crying.

Chapter 12.
Down the rabbit hole?

Today I decided to head down to the Os-yen
burrow as I wanted to send a letter to my family at
Unicorn Stables. I had written the letter last night
telling them all about my journey here and how my
Mystical Knight training was going well, I left out
the part about the shadow demons returning and
the strange dreams I had been having as I didn't
want to worry them. I had promised them I would
keep in touch as much as I can but as none of
them used magic, I couldn't use my S.C.D. I could
only send them letters.
I had looked at my map and seen the Os-yen
burrow was just past the stables, I was excited to
see what it looked like.

Though before I left I decided to go see Doctor
Wesley and Summer as I needed to get my eyes
checked, as one was still red, I would also get my
arm checked even though I already knew it had
healed.
I walked through the medical room doors and
Summer saw me.
  "Hello Rose, what can I help you with?" She
asked.

"Hello Summer, would it be alright for you to check
my eyes, one of them is still red after using too
much magic, it normally goes back to normal after
a day or two but this time it hasn't, also could you
check my arm has fully healed." I replied.
  "Of course, please take a seat and I will get the
Doctor too."

I sat down on an empty bed and Summer walked into the Doctor's office, after a short wait they both came back out to see me.

"Hello Rose, Summer has explained to me what the problem is, first she will check your arm and then we will both look at your eyes." Said Doctor Wesley.

I nodded and held out my arm. I had already removed the bandage; Summer used her fairy magic to check and make sure it had healed fully and right.

"Yes, your arm has fully healed and it's fine." Said Summer.

"Great, it is wonderful you heal like a shapeshifter, you are the only human I've heard of who can do this." Said the doctor.

"Thank you, I just wish my eye would go back to normal too." I said.

"Yes let us have a look." Doctor Wesley said and both him and Summer studied my eyes and Summer also used her fairy magic to see if anything was wrong.

"I can't see or feel anything wrong with your eye, only that it is a different color from the other one, isn't that right Doctor?" Said Summer.

"Yes, that is right, in fact you have perfect eyesight. If it is not hurting you and you said it has happened before, the only thing we can do is wait for it to go back to normal on its own, but I'm afraid it may even stay this color and in time maybe both eyes will become red. I'm sorry we can't help you more, but magic is unpredictable, and it has been

119

known to change appearances of the ones using it especially the ones using the strongest magical items." Explained Doctor Wesley.

"Don't worry though Rose, I'm sure you will be fine, and your red eye is pretty, you know some fairies and shapeshifters have different colored eyes too, so you won't stand out too much around here." Said Summer.

"Ok, thank you for your help." I said but I was still worried.

"Come back anytime Rose, to talk if you need too." Said Doctor Wesley.

"Alright, bye." I said and left the medical room.

On the way past the stables, I looked in the fields to see if I could see Silver, but I couldn't, he hadn't been in his stable either, I spotted Leah near the fence, so I went to ask her.

"Hi Leah, is Silver alright? I have not seen him."

"Hello Rose, I'm sorry I haven't seen him since last night." She replied.

"Oh, it's alright I'm sure he is around here somewhere, he's probably just gone for a walk." I said.

"Yes, it is probably for the best, I heard from Ethan he bit Declan last night."

"Oh no, I hope Declan is alright. I wonder why he doesn't like him, maybe he hasn't got used to all the new people yet."

"Declan is fine it wasn't a bad bite, and don't worry about Silver when he comes back, I will keep an eye on him for you." Said Leah.

"Thank you Leah, I'm off to post a letter then. Bye." I said and Leah nodded and waved at me as

I walked off.

I know I shouldn't worry about Silver as I know he
can take care of himself, but I still do, and I hoped
moving him here with me was the right choice.
I sighed and headed further down the track and
ended up in a wild meadow field, I spotted a small
house, so I walked over to it. I could already see
young Os-yens running about, they saw me
coming and hid behind a log. I smiled and waved
at them; they were very cute just like normal
bunnies, but I could sense their magical energy. I
continued to the house and knocked on the door,
a young girl opened it, she wore a name tag that
read Alice.

"Hello, I'm Rose and I'm here to see Matthew and
Alba. Are they here?" I asked.
    "Hello, it's nice to meet you, I'm Alice and yes
they are both here somewhere, come in and sit
down and I will get them for you." She replied.

I followed her inside and was shocked to see only
one room, it had a small unlit fireplace and
comfortable looking chairs all around. A Kings
Guard was sat in one of the chairs and it looked
like he was writing a letter, he looked up and
nodded at us, then he continued writing. I was
then more shocked to see four large holes in the
ground and when I looked closer, I realized there
were tunnels, and Alice disappeared down one of
them, so I sat down in one of the chairs and
waited.

A moment later Mathew appeared from the same
tunnel and said, "Hello Rose, come with me." He

turned back around, and I quickly got up to follow him.

"Normally only us who work here, and the Os-yen are allowed down here, but as you are new here you are allowed to come and have a look around, so I can explain how we send your letters and parcels and you can also see how the Os-yen live, I know seeing one was a shock to you so be prepared and don't stare too much." Explained Matthew and he smiled at me.

We walked further down the tunnel, and I realized it was lit up with light stones but also something else, Matthew saw me looking at them and explained.

"Those are called glow ores, they are like glow sticks but are not filled with fairy glitter to make them light up, they also don't need magic power to power them like the light stones, they glow in the dark and are normally only found in Os-yen burrows."

The glow ores were multicolored, and they reminded me of the jewel of darkness.

We came to a large opening into another room, and I gasped, children and Os-yen were sorting through piles of letters and boxes in a room that was set up like a school classroom.

"This room is where we sort through the letters and parcels, like a non-magic post office, we also have to make sure we put them in the right bags before they get taken through the right Os-yen portals to be closer to the places they need to go, and then we work in groups to deliver them. As only children and Os-yen can fit through the tunnels only we can do this, the other holes you saw in the first room lead to our living quarters, the Os-yen homes and the tunnel we all use to open up the Os-yen portals. Any questions?" Matthew asked me.

I shook my head and stared at the Os-yen working around the room.
   "Is this girl still staring at us?" Asked Alba who had come up beside us.
   "Ah sorry, I just think you are all wonderful." I replied as I looked all around again in awe.
   "Yes, we are." Said Alba and I thought I saw him smile a little.
   "Don't worry Rose I've lived here my whole life, and I'm still not used to seeing Matthew and Alba." Laughed Alice who had come over to see us.
   Matthew laughed and Alba sighed.

"So Rose is that letter for us to send?" Asked Matthew.
   "Ah yes but it is addressed to a place on the boarder of the non-magic realm, do you deliver that far out?" I asked and gave Matthew my letter.
   "Yes that will not be a problem, we deliver to a place not too far from there, and from there someone who lives in the non-magic realm takes over to deliver to non-magic places." Matthew explained as he read the address on the envelope.

"Thank you, I hear the portals you take go through the fairy realm, so you can get to places faster, is that true?" I asked.
   "Yes that is correct but don't expect a ride through, you are too tall, and Os-yen are not horses." Replied Alba and he took my letter from Matthew and stamped his front paw on it, a

magical symbol shaped like a paw appeared on
the envelope and lit up. He then carried the letter
to another child who was filling a bag up, the
young boy nodded and put my letter in the bag.

"The Os-yen stamp their paws onto the letters and
parcels so the receiver knows they came from
here, that bag will be going to the non-magic
realm. It should arrive to the right delivery person
tomorrow and then they will deliver it to the right
address in about three days and if the receiver
sends a reply back we will collect it the same way
and then me and Alba will bring it to your room."
Explained Matthew.

"Ah right, thank you." I said and smiled it sounded
like the Os-yen and the children worked very hard,
but I could tell they all had a close bond.
    "Right, I'm off to get some grass." Said Alba and
he started to hop off but before he could get to the
tunnel Matthew said,
    "Wait we will come too; I think Rose would like to
meet the others."

Alba nodded at him, and we followed him back up
the tunnel, on the way we passed three boys
carrying sacks they said hello and waved at us as
they passed us by and I read their name tags:
Logan, Oliver, and Thomas. It was definitely going
to be hard to remember everyone's names and
faces but I was going to try my best as I knew I
wanted to stay here.
We left the house and walked around to the back,
and I gasped as I spotted at least twenty or more
Os-yen hopping around the meadow and eating
the grass, they were all different sizes and colors

and there were even some younger ones around
them playing and chasing each other around the
adults, they all looked very happy, and I wondered
if they were all part of the same family.
Alba ran forward to catch up to the younger Os-
yen and he jumped playfully onto a small brown
and white one.
   "That's Oswald, Alba's baby brother." Laughed
Matthew.

We sat down on top of a small hill in the meadow
and watched the Os-yen, I had a big grin on my
face as I hadn't seen so many magical creatures
in one place before, Matthew and Alice laughed as
they saw how excited I looked.
A pretty white Os-yen ran towards Alice, and she
gave her a hug and said, "Hello Snow."

The younger Os-yen were shy at first but once
they realized we weren't a threat they got braver
and came closer to us to play, they started running
around us and we laughed as we watched them.
A few of the adults came to rest near us and
Matthew told me their names; Flower, Thumper,
Flopsy, Milly, Misty, Ginger, Bumble, Pippin and
Hop were the ones near us, and there was still
more, maybe I should write a list I thought as I
watched them.
   "Don't worry, you will get used to remembering
everyone's names, once you stay here long
enough we all become a part of the family." Said
Alice and she smiled at Matthew and Snow.

I smiled too but I knew it would take me longer to
fit in and be a part of the Mystical Knights.
I glanced back at the Os-yen beside us, and I

realized they were looking at the jewel of darkness with concern and I knew the hardest task for me was gaining everyone's trust, I knew not everyone will except me being here as even the magical creatures feared and hated the jewel of darkness and the one carrying it would always be known as being cursed.

I knew then if I didn't show everyone that I could control the magic within it and use it for good, I could not be a part of this family or become a Mystical Knight. This place could not become my home and I would be hated forever, thinking this made me feel sad again and I worried I would not be able to show everyone I was good enough.

Chapter 13.
Dangerous Magic.

"Ah, there you are Silver. I was wondering where you were, I hope you haven't been causing trouble." I said as I spotted Silver walking towards the stables.

I was on my way back from seeing the Os-yen and was heading to my afternoon lesson, as I patted his neck Silver nuzzled my arm expecting to find food.
"Alright I will bring you an apple next time but for now lets go and get you some hay." I said and laughed as he trotted behind me.

I decided to leave the pile of hay outside the stables so he could leave again and explore once he was finished; as I knew he liked to be out doors and free to do what he liked and unlike the other horses he could defend himself well against any creature in the forest or out run them if needed so I wasn't worried, also as he had bit Declan it was probably best he stayed away from him.
"Ok Silver, I have to go now, don't get into any trouble and stay close by, so I can find you tomorrow." I said.
Silver neighed and then carried on eating, and I knew he understood me and would do as I said.

The only lesson of the day was magic training; not all the students would be involved as the shapeshifters would be training later on in their animal form and Joseph and Liv didn't use a magical item. I will be training with Yara, Iris, some other fairies and a few of the Mystical Knights who did wield a magical item.

As I walked to the yard where the lesson would take place I felt nervous, I knew my magic was getting stronger as I felt it grow each day, but it was also becoming unpredictable. Nearly every night I had nightmares and when I woke up the jewel of darkness would be floating above my head and flashing all different colors, once it had even messed up my room and today it had even smashed the mirror hanging on my wall.

I was hoping magic training would help me control it better, but I had my doubts.

I got to the yard and stopped as I saw the crowd of people, it looked like most of the Kings Guards and the other students had decided to come watch us train.

I took a deep breath and entered the yard, I saw Edmund first, so I walked over to him.

"Hello Ed." I said.

"Ah hello Rose, have you placed your bets yet?" He asked and smiled.

"What?" I asked.

"Don't listen to him Rose he's an idiot." Said Marigold who had come to stand beside us.

"Ouch, you don't have to be so mean. Everyone can put bets on the person they think will be the best at using their magic, whoever guesses right will win the money and if more than one person gets it right their names will be put into a hat and the name that gets drawn out will get to keep all the money." Edmund explained.

Well, that explained the large crowd, I looked around at everyone talking and laughing together.

"Ok everyone settle down. Fairies and magical item users please come over here." Shouted a tall fairy with bright silver eyes and long dark brown hair that was neatly braided down one side of his head.

I walked towards him with Marigold and Edmund, Clover also ran out of the crowd to join us. I also spotted Iris, and Yara who I heard held a magical boomerang weapon.

"Right, today you will be aiming your magic towards the targets once they appear around the yard, one at a time the targets will pop up and you have to be fast to hit them however you also need to control your magic so you don't destroy them, just one hit of magic will knock the targets back down. This exercise will help with your concentration as you will need to learn how to use your magic around large crowds so you don't hurt innocent bystanders, the more you practice the easier it will get. Fairies will go first; Princess Marigold, I will let you show them how it is done." Marigold smiled and stood in the center of the yard while the rest of us left the arena to watch with the crowd.

The Fairy teacher stood next to me and said, "Rose, my name is Ainsley Wood, and I will be your magic training teacher. As you are new you can go last after watching the others, however I heard you have been training with Odin in the past so I'm sure you will be fine."

"Thank you, I will try my best." I replied and smiled.

Ainsley nodded and shouted back at Marigold, "Ok get ready."

He then put his arm up in the air and one by one

the targets popped up from the ground and
Marigold used her magical bracelet that was called
'Aquarius' to hit the targets with water and they fell
to the floor.

The crowd cheered and then the other fairies went
next along with Iris and Clover though they both
missed a few targets. Then it was Yara's turn, she
threw her magical boomerang weapon, and it
looked like she could control it with magic, it flew
through the air and hit every target, but it got stuck
in the last one and she had to go pull it out by
hand. Edmund went next he used his fire ring, he
also did well but got too carried away and burnt
the last target to ashes. The crowd cheered as
Marigold put the fire out with her magic, Edmund
smiled at Ainsley, but he looked annoyed and
shook his head.

Ainsley then turned to me and said, "Right, your
turn Rose."
  I nodded and headed to the middle of the arena
and the crowd fell silent.
Using my magic back home at Greenfield Village
had made my magic stronger and I had learnt to
use my magic without needing a weapon, I now
just used my hands to fire off magic in whatever
direction I pointed. I took a deep breath and
nodded at the Kings Guard who was controlling
the targets to let him know I was ready, Ainsley
shouted, "Go."

The first target rose from the ground, and I pointed
my hand at it, my magic shot the target back down
and the crowd cheered, I did this three more times
before realizing something felt off and my magic

was getting stronger. Another target popped up
and I fired off more magic but this time it didn't just
knock the target down, it destroyed it, along with
every other target that was on the ground before
they could even rise off the floor.

The crowd fell silent again as the arena burnt, I
looked at Ainsley but before I could apologize a
scream echoed around us and then shadow
demons appeared out of nowhere and started to
attack the crowd. The crowd yelled out and started
to fight back and some of the shapeshifters
changed into their animal forms to help. I fired off
more magic at a shadow demon getting too close
to the others but somehow it just made things
worse as more shadow demons appeared, I didn't
know what was happening and I didn't know what
to do, so I just stood in the center of the arena and
watched as everyone else fought off the demons
and for some reason I realized again not one of
the demons was coming after me.
  Some Kings Guards ran up to the others and
helped them fight and as the last of the demons
disappeared in a cloud of dust I noticed Marigold
use her water to put the fires out around the
targets. Everyone else stayed still as they
expected more shadow demons to come but none
came.

"Is everyone alright?" Shouted Ainsley.
  The crowd nodded and a few answered yes,
luckily no one had been hurt too badly during the
attack. I looked down at the jewel of darkness and
noticed it had turned a bright blue color.
  "What happened, where did they come from?" I
heard Joseph ask Ainsley.

Ainsley replied, "I'm not sure, something doesn't feel right about any of this."

"It is obvious, it all started when Rose used her magic!" Shouted Liv.

"I don't think…." Started Iris but Liv interrupted her and shouted.

"Oh, come on, she has that cursed item it is only a matter of time before she hurts someone or worse, she shouldn't be here."

"That's not true!" I yelled and the jewel of darkness flashed with sparks.

"Careful Rose." Said Ainsley.

I looked around at all the faces and saw fear in their eyes and I spotted a few Kings Guards raising their swords towards me as though I was going to attack them. I knew I had to leave so I turned around and ran towards the forest.

"Rose wait!" I heard Edmund shout, but I didn't stop I kept on running.

Chapter 14.
Meeting Tilly.

Surrounded by trees, alone in the forest, I took a deep breath and listened to the birds singing as I calmed down. I didn't care if being here was dangerous, I was angry and I knew if I didn't calm down the jewel of darkness would react and Liv would end up being right, I would hurt someone.
I felt confused too, I didn't know why the shadow demons kept appearing when I used my magic, was the jewel doing it or was it just a coincidence? I wondered should I stop using my magic altogether, but I knew from the past that was risky, if I bottled up my magic would it become too much for me?
With all these feelings and questions in my mind I walked deeper into the darkness of the trees.
Time ticked by and I wasn't sure how long I had been here, but I realized it had become colder and darker too.

I stopped and rubbed my hands together to warm them and decided I should probably head back when I suddenly realized I wasn't alone, out from behind a tree walked a beautiful woman in a long purple dress and as she got closer I realized she was a fairy. Her large gold eyes examined me.
   "You should not be here alone Rose." She said in a gentle voice.

"Who are you, and how do you know my name?" I asked and backed away slowly, as I got my dagger out from my belt and pointed it at her.
   "Do not worry, I am a friend. My name is Tilly,

and I know your friends Marigold and Clover.
Would you like to talk?" She said, then she sat
down near a tree.

"Um…I'm alright thanks." I replied.
"Now don't be shy Rose, you can talk to me. I
know you are feeling lost and alone and your
magic feels unbalanced, you need to talk to
someone about it otherwise it will overwhelm you
and you will lose control."

"I'm fine and you don't know me; I am stronger
than I look." I said and held my dagger tighter.

"I don't doubt your strength, just because you feel
sad does not mean you are weak. If you don't
want to talk to me about it, I understand but talking
to one of your friends will help you." Said Tilly and
she smiled.

Before I could reply I suddenly heard a rustle in
the bushes behind me, I spun around and smiled,
it was Silver.

"See, not all your friends need to talk back to you
but I'm sure they will still help." Said Tilly as I
stroked Silver's neck.
Silver nuzzled my arm and then he noticed Tilly,
he walked up to her, and she held out her hand to
his nose. Then Silver did something that shocked
me, he bowed at her. I have only seen him do that
to the judges at the end of a show jumping trial
and only when I have asked him to, and he didn't
do it often.

Tilly smiled then said, "More of your friends are
looking for you, you should go back home."

"Lately I'm not sure if this is the right home,
maybe I don't even belong here." I replied as
Silver walked back over to me.

"Don't worry Rose, soon you will realize this is the right place for you. This is your true home; you do belong here I can tell." She said.

Before I could reply I heard someone shouting, "Rose!" It was Odin.

"Rose, come back!" Shouted Edmund.

"Rose where are you; can you hear me?" Tristan's voice said in my mind.

I turned back to Tilly, but she was no longer there, she had gone.

I replied through our mind link, **"I'm alright Tristan, Silver is with me. I will make my way back to you, we are close."**

"Good." He said.

I followed Silver towards the others, even without Silver's help I would have found them as I could sense where they were. I saw Tristan first in his panther form, and he looked annoyed but also concerned when he spotted me. I smiled at him then I saw Layla coming towards me, she gently grabbed my hand with her mouth then she led me to Odin and Edmund.

"Thank goodness you are alright, do not run away like that again." Said Odin as he put his hand on my shoulder.

"Yeah Rose, we all know it wasn't you who summoned the shadow demons." Said Edmund.

"How do you know? What if it was my magic, I keep losing control." I said.

I felt a sharp pain on my hand as Layla bit down harder. "Ow."

"Layla please let go of Rose, she won't run away

135

again. Right?" Said Odin and he looked at me.

I nodded and Layla let go, I wiped the drool on my
trousers and smiled.
"Sorry I made you all worry."
 "That is alright, let's all go back now." Said Odin.
"Yeah, I need a drink, Silver can I get a lift?"
Asked Edmund.
Silver huffed, whipped his tail, and walked off.
Odin and I laughed.
 "Harsh." Said Edmund.
"Come on Rose, you look freezing lets get you
back home and I will get you some hot tea." Said
Odin.
I nodded and walked back with the others.

Once we got back to the tower I made my way to
Odin's office with Odin, Layla, and Edmund.
Tristan had left to change back into his human
form and change into some clean clothes but
before he left he told me off for running away
without him. Isabella had met us at the door and
told us she would go and get the food and drinks
and meet us back at the office.
I sat down in one of the chairs and sighed, my
body ached, and I was cold, and I could also feel
my magic sizzling through me as though it wanted
to be used again. I pushed it down, I would not
use my magic again, not until I figured out what
was wrong with it. Odin threw one of his blankets
at me, sat down on his large chair and smiled as
he watched me wrap myself up in it.

"Now we need to work out what happened during
the lesson and figure out where the shadow
demons came from." Said Odin.

"The first demon I saw came from behind the other students in the crowd." Said Edmund.

"Something felt off and when I used my magic the targets got destroyed and then I heard someone screaming and the others yelled out, I don't know who or what caused it." I explained.

"I see, so they just appeared again. My guess is they came out of a dark portal but normally a member of the Dark Shadow Guild has to be nearby, did both of you notice anyone new in the crowd, someone who didn't look like they belonged there?" Asked Odin.

"No, not that I remember but I was watching the magic lesson more than the crowd." Replied Edmund.

"I'm still learning everyone's names and faces so if there was someone new I wouldn't know." I said.

"Right, well we definitely need to stay alert, the Dark Shadow Guild is making a move, we just have to figure out what they are planning." Said Odin.

There was a knock at the door and Isabella walked in with Tristan back in human form, and Marigold and Clover, they were carrying trays full of food and drinks. As they put them down on the desk Edmunds stomach rumbled loud and we all laughed.

"Sounds like we came just in time." Said Clover and Edmund laughed as he grabbed a sandwich. Tristan smiled and handed me a cup of warm tea.

"Thank you." I said and the others sat down in the other chairs around the room.

The others grabbed some food off the trays.

"We need to keep an eye out for anything suspicious, if the Dark Shadow Guild is making another move to take the jewel of darkness or another magical item we need to be prepared." Said Odin, and he handed some chicken over to Layla.

"I agree, they have stayed quiet for a while so them appearing now must mean they have something planned." Said Isabella.

"Yeah, there haven't been many sightings of shadows around here, we haven't had to fight so many since that time at Greenfield Village, I was hoping they quit after Caleb was…Um gone." Said Edmund and he glanced at me.

I looked down at my drink and thought, so basically ever since I got here there has been more shadow demons and more people in danger, maybe I was a curse. Maybe my magic was the cause of this problem.

A tray of food appeared in front of me.

"You should eat too Rose." Said Clover.

I smiled and took a sandwich off the tray,

"Ok, thank you." I said.

"The fairies have said they have sensed more darkness in the area, so they are keeping watch and patrolling more in the forests." Explained Marigold.

"Yeah I saw a fairy in the forest earlier just before Silver found me, she seemed nice. She said her name was Tilly." I said after I swallowed a bite of the sandwich.

The room went silent, and I noticed the others looked shocked.

"What's wrong?" I asked.

"Are you sure she said Tilly?" Asked Odin.

"Yes, why? Who is she?"

"I can't believe it, she's back." Whispered Marigold.

"Yay, Auntie is back." Shouted Clover.

"Tilly is the fairy Queen; her full name is Titania Topaz. She has been away from the fairy realm for a while, but no one knows why, I guess she decided it was time to come back." Explained Isabella.

The fairy realm is on the outskirts of Sunlight City in the forest, but you can only visit there if a fairy goes with you as only fairy magic can open the gates. Fairies can also travel through any tree from anywhere in the magic realm to get there.

"Oh, I do hope I didn't disrespect her I really need to be told who royalty is around here, pointing my dagger at the fairy queen probably wasn't the best idea and I keep forgetting Tristan is now the prince." I said and covered my face with my hand.

The others laughed and Edmund said, "Don't worry Rose I always forget to bow too, and I've beaten Tristan plenty of times, though even I wouldn't get on the wrong side of the fairy queen, she's tough."

"Yes, don't worry Rose I won't punish you, but Edmund might be in trouble." Smiled Tristan.

I laughed as Edmund hid behind Marigold and smiled as I realized even though we haven't been together much since I moved to Sunlight City I could always count on my friends for support.

We sat for a while eating and talking together then
Marigold and Clover decided to leave and go to
the fairy realm to see if the queen had returned.
Tristan and Edmund decided to play a game of
chess while Odin and Isabella made plans for our
trip during tomorrows magic history lesson. Layla
fell asleep and I decided to read a book Odin had
given me, on the history of fairy royalty, it was an
interesting read, but as I was reading my eyes
started to close and I drifted off into a deep sleep.

I woke up sometime later and realized only myself
and Tristan was in the room; he was sat at Odin's
desk reading a book.
He looked up when he heard me move and
smiled. "You should go to bed if you're tired." He
said.

I yawned and asked, "Where did everyone go,
how long was I asleep?"
   Tristan replied with concern, "The others have
gone to bed; you've been asleep for about two
hours. You didn't even wake up when Edmund
banged the door closed, you must have been
tired."
   "Yeah I guess walking around the forest tired me
out." I smiled and stretched my arms.
   "That is not the only reason though, is it? You
have not been sleeping well, you have been
having nightmares again, right?"

I looked at Tristan shocked, how did he know? but
then I remembered as our minds are connected
with our mind link, he knew when I was troubled.
Once in the past I had opened my mind link during
one of my nightmares and screamed and he had

come running thinking I was in real trouble. I
hoped I hadn't done it again.

"Sorry, I haven't woken you up, have I?" I said
and pointed at my forehead.

"No but I have been sleeping in the castle more
than the tower so maybe your dreams haven't
reached me yet. Do you want to talk about it?"

I wondered if I should tell Tristan about my
nightmares and about the Dark Shadow Guild, the
death of Caleb's sister or even about Caleb's
ghost haunting me, and should I even tell him
about Lucas coming back, and that I can now see
him without the need of a reflection.
I decided not to though, as it wasn't the right time
and he had his own problems of dealing with
becoming the official Prince of Sunlight City, I
couldn't burden him with my problems too.

"No, it's fine, it is just taking me longer to settle
into my new home. I'm sure I will be fine in a
couple of days, so don't worry." I told him instead.

"I always worry, but if you change your mind, you
know where to find me if you want to talk." He said
and I could tell he knew something was bothering
me, other than being in a new home.

"Thank you Tristan, I know I can count on you but
I'm fine really. I should probably go to bed though
and you should too, we have a hard day planned
tomorrow." I said and stood up.

"Ok. I will soon, goodnight Rose." Said Tristan.

"Goodnight Tristan." I said, then I walked out the
door.

Chapter 15.
The trip to Sun Star Cave.

As I walked to the stables I looked around at all the pretty flowers that had bloomed, the temperature was warm today but luckily not uncomfortable so it would be a nice day to go for a ride out. Today we were going on a training exercise and camping out overnight, a part of me was excited about the adventure but the other part was worried about staying out overnight as my nightmares had gotten worse.

I smiled as I found Silver standing next to Patrick, Ethan was tacking Patrick up and I noticed Silver's tack hanging on the fence beside him.
  "Good morning Ethan." I said and patted both horses on their necks.
  "Ah, morning Rose, are you alright to tack Silver up? Declan tried but Silver wouldn't let him go near him and he's been feisty today he only calmed down once Declan left and I brought Patrick over to him." He said.
  "Yes of course, we should help you tack our horse's up when we can, and I know Silver can be a handful sometimes." I smiled as Silver butted his head against my arm in protest.

As I groomed and tacked him up I spotted the other students standing to one side talking and packing their bags while waiting for their horses to be tacked up by Leah, George, and Declan. Declan glanced at me and for a moment I saw a glimpse of hatred in his eyes, and I wondered why he didn't like me, was it because I had the jewel of darkness or was it something else, and maybe that is why Silver didn't like him, maybe he could sense his hatred towards me. Before I could think about it more, I saw Odin, Tristan, Isabella, and Dominic heading towards the other students, so I quickly finished tacking Silver up.

Once Silver was done I started to pack my extra supplies into the saddle bags, during breakfast we had been giving extra packs of food to help us on our journey.

"Are you ready Rose?" Asked Isabella as she walked towards me.

"Yes, I'm all set to go." I replied and I gathered Silver's reins in my hands and jumped up onto his back.

"Good, it is time to go, we will be following Dominic, are you ready Tristan?" She asked, as Tristan took Patrick's reins from Ethan and nodded his thanks.

"Yes, let's go, before Vincent sees me." Replied Tristan.

"Tristan I thought you were supposed to tell him you are coming with us." Said Isabella.

"If I did I knew he would try to call the whole thing off, besides, I need a break from all the drama." Sighed Tristan.

"Yes, and there is no better way to take a break than camping with your best mates beside a warm fire, drinking, eating and dancing." Said Edmund as he walked his horse up beside us.

"Really boys, this isn't a holiday." Isabella sighed and she walked off to get her horse. I laughed as Edmund winked at me.

There was a flash of light beside Odin as Dominic changed into his wolf form, he and Isabella will be

in charge today as Odin decided it would be best
to stay behind as he needed to be in charge while
the king and Tristan were away, and he wanted to
keep an eye out for any shadow demon activity
while we were gone.

Odin stepped forward and shouted.

"Alright everyone, it is time for you to go, you all
have maps if you become separated but it would
be best for all of you to stay together as a group
so you can practice working as a team. Dominic
will be in the lead if any of you need to stop for a
rest make sure you let the others know. If
everyone is ready, please mount your horses and
follow Dominic."

As the others mounted their horses and started to
follow Dominic, Odin walked over to me and said,

"Please be careful and if you need anything
please ask Isabella or Dominic for help. And
remember keep your guard up but don't use your
magic unless you absolutely have to, I don't want
the Dark Shadow Guild tracking your location. And
Layla you be good too."

I looked down beside me and smiled, Layla was
sat waiting for us, it looked like she wanted to
come too.

"Alright, don't worry we will be fine. See you
when we get back." I replied and waved at him as
Silver followed the others through the gate and
into the forest.

The other students on their horses stayed at the
front with Isabella and Dominic but I stayed with
Layla, Tristan, Edmund, and Gray. Jaxon was
behind us in his wolf form, the Kings Guards had
to stay with Tristan at all times. I still found it funny
that the Mystic Council thought a panther needed

protection.

I noticed some of the students had turned around to look at us and they looked annoyed, I could tell they were mad I was still allowed to come, as they still believed I was responsible for the shadows attacking yesterday. They had also avoided me at breakfast, so I had eaten mine alone in the indoor garden while reading the book on the Dark Shadow Guild until Edmund had found me.

I knew I needed to find out where the shadow demons were coming from and why they were coming now and also find out who was really controlling them so I could help the Mystical Knights protect everyone, but for now I should just enjoy this ride and hope everything will be alright. Yesterday we were told we would be riding through the forest and across the moors to a cave where in the past a magical item had been found. Isabella and Dominic were going to show us the location so we could learn and know what to expect in the future when we would become fully trained Mystical Knights and have to go off to find other magical items.

The ride through the forest was uneventful and we only stopped twice to have a rest. We had gone down a different path than the one before and it was great seeing all the huge trees that looked like they had been around for hundreds of years. We had also seen deer, boars and even a fox but they soon ran off once they saw us coming.

Once we got out of the forest the shapeshifters of the group decided to dismount their horses and change into their animal form so they could run over the moors. The open land was vast in front of us, and I could sense Silver also wanted to run.

"Easy boy, not yet." I said.

I made sure Patrick was still with Edmund as the
shapeshifter's horses had to follow the rest of us.
Tristan, Jaxon, Gray, Jasper, T.J., and Layla
followed Dominic over the moors at a steady run.
It was weird seeing five wolves, a bear and a
panther running together.

"Alright everyone, we will also quicken our pace
but try to stay together." Shouted Isabella and she
sent her horse into a canter and the rest of us
followed behind her.
We stayed together but I felt Silver wanted to go
faster so I let him, he took off and galloped past
the others.

"Hey! Slow down." Shouted Liv but we ignored
her and carried on.

I laughed as we quickened our pace and I
spotted the shapeshifters running in front, we soon
caught up to them and Silver kept up with them
easily but then he decided to run past them, and I
could tell he was having fun, so I let him.
A moment later I decided we should slow back
down and wait for the others to catch up, as I
didn't want to get lost.

"Whoa boy, we better let the others catch up." I
said and Silver started to slow back down into a
walk.

"You just wanted to have some fun, right Silver." I
laughed and patted him on the neck.

Silver neighed in delight, and I smiled, even
though we had travelled a good distance and he
had ran fast he was hardly showing any signs of
being tired, he has always had good stamina and
speed and that was another reason people
thought he was a magical horse.

The shapeshifters caught up and Tristan said in my mind, "**Wow, I forgot how fast Silver can run.**"

I looked down at Tristan, smiled and said out loud, "Yep we haven't ran that fast in a while, I think he enjoyed it."

Dominic growled and continued past us, and the others followed him, I guess that meant follow me. We were heading towards some trees in the distance it looked like another forest, the others with their horses soon caught up to us.

Isabella smiled at me and said, "Wait for us Rose."

I laughed and we all followed Dominic through the trees to a clearing and on the other side was a large cave. It had two large stone pillars on each side of the entrance and the remains of some old forgotten steps leading up to the entrance. We dismounted our horses and in a flash of light the shapeshifters changed back into their human forms and quickly put their clothes back on.

"Alright everyone, let's take care of the horses and get them settled down." Shouted Dominic.

We unloaded the bags and hay from the horse's backs and untacked them, then we gave them some hay and while the horses settled down, one by one we followed Dominic and Isabella to the entrance of the cave.

"This is Sun Star Cave, it used to be a home for the Sunne Tribe who used it during the summer months, we came across it when the fairies told us there was a magical presence nearby. We found the magical item the Ra Stone." Explained Isabella.

We walked into the cave, inside was large and it

smelt of damp moss. In the middle of the cave stood a pedestal with red glyphs all around it, in front of it was a small fire pit that the tribe must have used to keep warm. Isabella walked up to the pedestal and pointed to it.

"This is where the Ra Stone was, as you can see we had to decipher the glyphs and symbols to make sure we could remove the item safely and without causing harm to the area, as some magical items can also be surrounded by traps or curses. We had to turn the symbols to the correct points to remove the stone safely, otherwise this would happen." Said Isabella and she nodded at Dominic.

He took his sword out of his sheath and gently moved a symbol on the pillar, then he moved away fast as spikes flew out of the stone that could do some serious damage to anyone who was standing too close.
The other students gasped, and Edmund whistled.
"This is also why it's important to study your different languages and culture and why it's better to work as a team so you can support each other as you travel to different locations to find magical items. Now I want you to study the symbols and draw the pedestal in your books, write down what you think the symbols mean and remember look, don't touch." Explained Isabella.

We all settled down around the pedestal with our notebooks and did what was instructed, Layla fell asleep while the rest of us worked. I glanced up and looked towards the entrance of the cave and spotted Tristan, Edmund and Dominic setting up camp outside as we will be sleeping outside tonight around the fire, and as they were already Mystical Knights they didn't need to study like us as they had done it before during their own training.

I decided to draw the pedestal first then work out what the symbols mean, it was difficult for me as growing up in the non-magic realm at Greenfield Village we never got taught about the different languages and cultures of the magic realm so figuring out which languages the symbols were from was hard work but with the help of my book and Isabella, I managed.

After a while Tristan and Edmund came back to the cave to rest and the rest of us finished with our work.

"Right, well done everyone. Most of you have worked out what the symbols mean, top marks go to Joseph who got them all right on his own. Joseph, please explain to the others what the symbols mean." Said Isabella.

"Alright, the top of the pedestal explains about the Ra Stone, it says 'the Ra Stone that shines like the sun and keeps us warm, will give life to those who wield it.' The next part warns if it is to be removed from the pedestal by the wrong kind, danger awaits, and it can bring harm." Explained Joseph.

"Yes, that's it, as you heard the Ra Stone gives off light like the light stones, but it also gives off heat, the Sunne Tribe found the cave and worshipped the stone and gave it the name, as in their culture their sun God is named Ra. It stayed in this cave for many years as the Sunne Tribe lived here but due to the dangers of the Dark Shadow Guild wanting more magical items and due to the tribe moving to a new location, a place now called Sunna village; it was decided by the king the Ra Stone would also move to a new location to keep it safe." Explained Isabella.

"So where is the Ra Stone now?" Asked Iris. "Well, some of the ancestors of the Sunne Tribe keep it in a secret location, even I don't know where that is but we make sure we keep in touch so they can inform us if anything changes." Answered Isabella.

"That is a shame, it would have been nice to see it." Said Iris.

"Yes, I would have liked to see it to." Said Joseph.

"Yes I understand, but as you know a few magical items are kept in secret locations around our realm to keep them safe, we can't see them all but once you become Mystical Knights there are some you can see and some of you may receive a magical item of your own, though I know two of you already have one." Said Isabella and she smiled at me and Yara.

"Yeah, though not all of them are good to have." Said Liv and she glared at me.

Before Isabella could reply, Jasper asked, "Is that supposed to be a dragon on the bottom." And he pointed at the bottom of the pedestal. There was a symbol of a winged creature, and it did look like a dragon.

"Yes, it is believed to be a dragon and that is why the Sunne Tribe decided to stay here as they worship the dragons, the Ra Stone is their symbol of hope and life. I can't show you the real stone, but I can show you a photo of it in our next lesson when we return home." Explained Isabella.

Dominic and Jaxon walked back into the cave and Layla woke up, and she stretched her front paws out and looked at us.

"Isabella the fire is lit for you. Have you finished with your lesson?" Asked Dominic.

"Ah yes, thank you." Said Isabella.
"Good, Tristan, go ahead and tell the others what they need to do now." Said Dominic.

"Right. As Mystical Knights you sometimes have to travel to new places and when you do, you don't always have the option to stay at an inn so you need to camp out and learn the skills you need, so I will put you in groups to do some jobs. Isabella will be making the dinner, so I want Liv and Iris to help her. Rose and Yara you will both make sure the horses have everything they need. Jasper, T.J., and Joseph will be coming with me, and with Edmund, and Layla to do a patrol around camp and make sure the area is safe from predators and other unwanted guests. Dominic will stay around camp and help anyone who needs it." Explained Tristan.

We all nodded and walked out of the cave to start our jobs. Yara and I worked well together, even though she didn't speak much we managed to fill up an old stone water trough using the nearby well and we made sure the horses had enough hay from the sack we had brought with us, the horses could also move around the small fenced in area they were in and eat some of the grass. Dominic had told us, sometimes areas Mystical Knights travel to, can have nearby supplies at hand for themselves and for their horses but sometimes you can be alone and you have to work out the best way to keep yourself and your horse looked after, sometimes it was also better to keep your horses tacked up if you knew you had to make a swift exit or you weren't staying long. Tonight though our horses would stay untacked so we carried their tack to the cave with the other supplies.

After a while Tristan came back from patrolling with the others, they had not seen any unwanted guests, so it was safe to camp here, we all settled down around the fire and ate the wonderful chicken stew that Isabella had made with the help of Liv and Iris. Isabella had brought the ingredients with us today but as we ate, she explained that sometimes you would have to find food from the land around you as you wouldn't always have the option of bringing food with you or going to the nearby markets so it was important we learn more about what we can eat in the wild. Once we had finished with our food, Dominic and Isabella explained more about camping out and showed us nearby mushrooms and berries we could eat if we needed to find food, we all made notes, and I hoped I could remember everything we were being taught.

We all set up our sleeping bags around the fire and as Jaxon stood guard in his wolf form, one by one everyone else fell asleep under the stars, but I kept my eyes open and watched the fire flicker and burn and I wondered if I would be able to become an official Mystical Knight, as these thoughts moved around my head, my eyes drifted shut.

Chapter 16.
When Darkness Falls.

"Rose!"
Someone was yelling my name but all I could see was darkness.

"Rose, Wake Up!" I knew that voice, someone was shaking me, and I heard a wolf howl. My eyes flickered open, and I saw Tristan's green eyes looking at me with concern.

"What?" I mumbled.
"Wake up Rose, look up." He said and something in his voice made me open my eyes wider, he sounded scared.

I looked up and saw the jewel of darkness floating above my head but not just that, my dagger was also next to it, pointing down above my chest. I sat up and looked around and I noticed everyone else was stood near the entrance of the cave with fear in their eyes, and I realized why. Everyone had weapons hanging above their sleeping bags ready to fall down and stab them!

"Rose, the jewel!" Shouted Isabella who was stood with the others.

I looked up again and realized it was the jewel of darkness that was doing this, I felt its magic wrapped around the weapons.

"**Rose, are you alright?**" Asked Tristan through our mind link.

I nodded at him and grabbed the jewel, as I did all the daggers and swords fell from the sky and just in time Tristan grabbed my bag and blocked the dagger from hitting me.

Someone screamed, we looked and noticed Liv
had gone back to her sleeping bag at the wrong
time and her dagger had cut her arm. The others
ran to her, and I slowly got to my feet, I looked
down at the jewel in my hand, it was glowing a
bright red and I wondered what had happened for
it to react like that.

   "She shouldn't be allowed to train with us, she's
dangerous, she could have killed us all." Shouted
Liv.

   I looked up and noticed Isabella trying to wrap a
bandage around Liv's arm.
I slowly walked over to them and held my hand out
towards them and said, "Here let me heal you, I
can fix your arm."

   "Stop, stay away from me. You have caused
enough damage!" Yelled Liv and she backed away
from me.

   "I'm sorry I don't know what happened." I said.
"Just stay away from me." Whispered Liv and she
slowly sat down on the ground.

   "You will be alright Liv." Said Joseph. And the
others gathered around her.

I took a deep breath and walked away from them
and headed towards the horses, luckily no
weapons had been near them, so they were
alright. The sun had just started to light the sky up
and the air smelt damp, it felt like it was going to
rain. Silver walked up to me, and he nuzzled his
nose up against my head, he was worried about
me. I smiled and stroked his neck, then I shivered
as a cold wind started to blow, I had left my cloak
near my sleeping bag.

   "I hope you're not planning on leaving without
me." Said Tristan as he walked up to us with Layla

following him. I also spotted Jaxon and Gray standing close by, I guess they no longer trusted me with the prince.

I shrugged my shoulders and said, "Not yet." Tristan sighed and handed me my cloak that he had brought with him.

"Thanks" I said.

"If you leave, so will I." He said.

I smiled as Layla rubbed her head against my leg.

"So, what happened?" Asked Tristan.

I wrapped my cloak around me and replied. "I don't know, I was having a nightmare and I guess the jewel must have reacted. Sorry."

"Are you alright though, did something hurt you?" He asked with concern.

"Yes I'm alright just shocked, and thanks to you nothing hurt me, if you had not been here…. Well, I hate to think what would have happened, Liv is right I shouldn't have come."

"Rose, magic is unpredictable anyone can have problems with it. You have the burden of carrying the jewel of darkness not everyone can do it and I think you're doing a great job; you have saved plenty of people with your magic so don't let anyone judge you because of your mistakes or accidents, I know plenty who have had a lot more than you." Said Tristan.

I smiled, Tristan has always been someone I can count on to cheer me up and give me good advice, just like his brother.

Before I could reply I noticed Edmund had come up behind us and he said, "Wow that was a great speech prince, did you read that from a book?" And he laughed.

"And here is a perfect example of someone who has made many mistakes." Smiled Tristan.

"Ouch, Rose I think you need to heal my heart with your magic, Tristan has just broke it." Said Edmund and he placed his hands over his heart and then fell to the floor and rolled about.

I laughed as Tristan walked back to the camp fire shaking his head. I knew they were both trying to cheer me up and it worked.

"Thank you." I said, I saw Tristan nod his head as he heard me.

"Why are you thanking him, I am being serious I need help." Said Edmund and I laughed as Layla jumped on him.

"Not even my magic can help you." I laughed and I headed back to my sleeping bag.

My smile soon faded once I saw the other students looking at me with fear and anger in their eyes. I sat down and watched Isabella as she boiled some water to make us all a hot drink, I was still tired, but I knew I wouldn't be able to go back to sleep so I got the book on the shadows out my bag to read but before I could even open the book, shadow demons in the shape of humans appeared from behind the trees and surrounded us. Layla and Gray who was now in his wolf form howled, the other shapeshifters changed into their animal forms in a flash of light and pounced.

"Grab your weapons!" Yelled Isabella.

She ran to the cave with the others, and I realized they were trying to get their weapons; they must have put them in the cave so my magic wouldn't control them again. I took my dagger from its sheath on my belt and thrust it up towards a shadow that had ran at me then I tried to defend the others as they received their weapons back, I also grabbed my katana sword. Once everyone was armed, we started to fight off the shadow demons, I didn't want to use my magic as I feared it would get out of control, so I used my sword instead.

Another demon charged at me, and I managed to fight it off and as it vanished in black smoke I ran at another one to attack, the next one was also defeated but as I turned to attack again, one jumped at me from the side and collided into me. I landed on the floor and gasped then quickly rolled out of the way as it tried to stab me with its sword, Tristan tore through it and came to stand beside me as I got back up to my feet.

"Circle formation!" Yelled Edmund as he took another demon out with a fire ball that shot out of his fire ring.

We all gathered around in a circle and stood back-to-back so we could defend each other, just how we practiced during training. It was a good strategy and one by one the demons fell. The last shadow left the camp and disappeared into a black mist.

"Well, that was fun." Said Edmund as he stretched his arms.

"Is everyone alright?" Asked Isabella.

"Yeah, I think so." Said Joseph as he checked a cut on his arm.

"No, not really. This whole exercise has been a joke, wait until my father hears about this!" Said Liv angrily, and I remembered hearing her father was the head of the Mystic Council.

"Right, I think it is time for us to head back home,

shapeshifters should stay in their animal form until we arrive back in case any more shadow demons appear, the rest of us will get the horses ready to leave." Said Isabella and she sighed.

We quickly got to work packing up the bags and tacking up the horses but at every sound we heard we became quiet and got ready for another fight but in the end it was just another forest animal or bird, the shapeshifters patrolled around us to make sure it was safe. I looked at the spot the last shadow demon had been and wondered why they had come, were they still after me and the jewel again or was it something else, one minute they would attack me, or leave me and attack others nearby. It was confusing. I felt a wet nose touch my hand, it was Layla, and I could tell she was worried about me.

"I'm alright Layla, are you, you didn't get hurt did you?" I asked.

Layla ran around me and made a yapping noise, and I guessed that meant she was fine.

Once everyone was ready, we all mounted the horses and followed the shapeshifters back, we all stayed quiet and I could tell everyone was nervous, even the horses knew something was wrong, we all stayed together so we could keep each other safe. We could all sense danger was approaching.
We made it back over the moorlands without problems but as we entered the forest the rain started to fall and something didn't feel right, then we heard drumming sounds and then the shadow demons appeared again.

"Everyone hurry get back to the tower!" Yelled

Isabella.

The horses picked up the pace and the shapeshifters stayed beside us to block any attacks. We all managed to stay together and made it back to the path that led to the gate, I quickly glanced behind us and noticed how many shadow demons were behind us, there were too many. I knew what to do to stop them, I asked Silver to slow down, he wasn't happy about it, but he listened, and I jumped off him and turned around to face the shadow demons. A wolf and a panther suddenly came to stand beside me, and they both looked angry, and I wasn't sure if it was at me or the demons.

I yelled, "Don't worry, I have a plan."

Then I slammed my hands to the ground and used the spell of protection.

My magic shield grew around us and blocked the shadow demons from moving closer, the shadows hissed out in pain as they tried to break the barrier but not one of them could. I felt my magic grow and my shield spread far and wrapped around the tower and king's castle. I smiled as I stopped my magic, I was glad I could protect everyone and I knew my magic shield would stay up a while, but my smile soon faded as something didn't feel right, I felt drained, my energy started to fade, and I felt dizzy. I felt Layla's mouth grab my arm as she tried to help me, and I heard Tristan's voice.

He said, **"Rose, what's wrong?"**

I felt myself fall and my eyes shut; I was in the darkness once more.

Chapter 17.
Change.

I was in a grey room with dark spirals swirling around me, I stood there feeling weak and alone. I didn't know where I was or why I was here, but I knew it wasn't a good place, something didn't feel right, I had to leave.
Crash!

That was the first sound I heard, I quickly opened my eyes and saw the jewel of darkness floating above my head, it was sparkling a bright blue color which usually happened when I was worried about something. I sat up, took the jewel in my hand, and realized I was in the medical room and my magic had just smashed the nearby mirror.

"Stop that! You should not use magic here." Shouted Stella who was stood beside another bed with a Kings Guard lying down in it, he had his eyes open and was looking at me with a worried expression.
   Layla suddenly appeared, jumped on my bed, and then started to growl at the nurse.
   Stella looked scared, she whispered to the Kings Guard, "I will go and get help." And then she ran out of the room.
   I said, "Easy Layla, I'm alright."
Then I gently put my hand out towards her, she nuzzled her nose up against it, then laid down next to me and I was glad the bed was large, as I would have fell off a normal sized bed and I realized the beds must be large in case any shapeshifters needed to use them.

"Is everyone else alright?" I asked her.

She licked my hand, and I somehow knew she meant yes.

"I bet your father is mad at me again." I laughed and we both looked up as we heard the door open.

Stella walked back in, followed by Odin and Doctor Wesley, they both looked at the smashed mirror and then looked at me and Layla.

"See, look what she did." Said Stella and Layla growled at her again.

"That's enough Layla, so what happened?" Asked Odin as he sat down in the chair next to my bed.

I explained, "I just had a bad dream, I'm sorry." And looked at Doctor Wesley who had grabbed a broom and was sweeping up the glass.

"It's alright, accidents happen." Said the Doctor. Stella shook her head and walked off.

"Do you feel alright now Rose?" Asked Odin. I nodded, took a sip from the glass of water beside my bed and put it back.

"It was reckless of you to use your magic again; you know it's getting stronger and harder to control. Your body might not be able to cope with it for much longer, you need to be more careful." Said Odin.

"I know that! It's my body, I feel everything, all the pain, all the magic and all the power. Every day I'm trying to keep it under control, and I'm scared I won't, and I will end up killing someone else. No one here knows how to help me; everyone just looks at me with fear and anger and I don't blame them I feel the same way about myself!" I yelled.

Odin held out his hand to touch mine. "Rose….I…"

I shouted, "Don't touch me!" And the glass of water beside my bed smashed.

Layla whimpered and put her paw on my hand and tears welled up in my eyes.

"I'm sorry, I need some space to clear my head." I said and I climbed out of bed.

I felt dizzy but luckily it didn't last, and I grabbed my cloak from the hook on the wall and quickly put my belt back on and made sure my katana sword was still in the sheath.

"Rose you need to rest." Said Odin.

The door flew open, and Councilor Vincent walked in with Tristan and his two guards behind him, I saw the councilor look at the smashed mirror and at Doctor Wesley who had just finished sweeping it up.

He yelled, "What happened, who did this, did the shadows attack again?"
I started to walk towards the door, Layla decided to follow me, but I didn't mind.

"Rose…Wait…," Before Odin could finish, Councilor Vincent interrupted him.

"Where are you going?" He asked me.
"Out, away from here. I have had enough time with people who hate me." I replied and marched out the door with Layla before anyone could stop me.

"**I don't hate you Rose, and you know there are many here who don't too**." Said Tristan through our mind link.

I rubbed the tears from my eyes and replied, "**I know, thanks.**"
Then I walked out the tower doors.

I headed to the forest a place I knew would calm

my mind. The forest was wet after the rain, but I
knew walking would help me and being away from
the crowds of people helped too. I must have been
asleep a while as it was already late in the
afternoon, Layla had followed me, and I could tell
she was worried about me. I stopped, turned
around and knelt down to face her.

"I'm glad you came with me, but you don't have
to stay if you don't want to." I told her.

Layla sat down in front of me, and I knew she
wasn't going to leave me.

"Thank you." I smiled.

I had planned to stay close to the tower but as we
set off walking again we ended up taking a
different path from the one before and to my
surprise I could hear running water, there was a
river nearby. I decided to keep following Layla as I
was curious on where this path would lead.

Once I got around the corner I looked down to my
left and noticed the river below us, I didn't realize
we had climbed so high. Further along Layla
stopped and sat down near the ledge where you
could see further across on the other side, it was a
nice peaceful place to have a rest and even
though I was scared of deep water, the sound of it
running down stream helped calm my mind. I
decided I would rest here a while with Layla but
before I could sit down beside her, I felt a strong
dark presence and so had Layla, she jumped up
and growled at something behind me.

I spun around, and out from behind the trees Finn
appeared with shadow demons beside him. I drew
my sword from my belt and moved closer to Layla.
I hadn't seen Finn since the incident at Greenfield
Village and he looked angry, I still remember him

shouting I would pay for what I had done to Caleb.

"Just like old times, except you are now with a mongrel instead of a kitten. Why don't we see how much your magic has grown." He said and smiled.

I knew if I used any more magic I would be in trouble so as the demons attacked, I used my sword to fight them off and it helped I had a wolf by my side, Layla took them out with ease.

"Come on Rose you can do better than that, the jewel of darkness should be used. I want to see your magic." Laughed Finn.

"Shut up!" I yelled, and the jewel fired off sparks of magic towards Finn, he easily jumped out of the way, and I became dizzy again.

"The boss wants you to join us, but I know the truth, you don't deserve to be in our guild. What you did to Caleb is unforgivable I won't allow you to be one of us. This all ends now!" Yelled Finn and he raised his arm up in the air.

I quickly took out another demon only to be pushed back by another and then a shadow demon shaped like a large bear slammed into my side and I was knocked off the edge of the cliff. I managed to grab onto the ledge with one hand and I dug my dagger into the side of the cliff, but I could feel it wouldn't hold for long, I was slipping and the sound of running water below made me panic.

"Layla!" I yelled.

Suddenly there was a flash of white light above me and then a girls face I had only seen in a photo appeared over the edge and she grabbed my hand with hers and pulled me up.

We both scrambled away from the edge, and I quickly looked around us; we were alone, Finn and the shadows had gone.

"Layla?" I said and looked at the girl, she was sat on the floor beside me and was watching me with her bright orange eyes.

She nodded and tried to speak but for some reason she couldn't, I quickly removed my cloak and handed it to her so she could cover up.
Layla had finally changed back into a human, and she had done it to save me.

"Thank you Layla, I owe you." I said.
She nodded again and tried to stand but her legs wobbled, I wondered if it was because she hadn't been a human in a while. I bent down next to her and said,

"Why don't we head back to the tower, I'm sure your father will want to see you. Here let me help you." I held out my hand towards her and she took it and smiled.

I helped pull her up to her feet and together we walked slowly back towards the tower. Layla had the same-colored hair as Odin, but it was long and matted due to her not been able to brush it or cut it while she was a wolf, her face also looked like his, but she had the same eyes and slender build as her mother which I remembered from a photo Odin had shown me. As we walked, Layla started to walk better but she still held onto me for support as she was still unsure.
We finally got back to the gate out of breath, and I wished I had brought Silver with us as he would have been a big help.
The guard waved us through the gate but then he stopped and dropped the pen he was holding as he noticed who was standing next to me, he must have known Layla as a human in the past and

165

remembered her. He grabbed an S.C.D. from his belt and started to shout through it.

"Odin, you need to come to the forest gate immediately."

After a short pause he said, "No, no you have to see this for yourself, I can't believe it!"
I looked at Layla and we both smiled.

A crowd of people suddenly appeared from behind the greenhouses, and they were heading in our direction. I noticed Odin, Isabella, and Tristan in the crowd. I felt Layla tense up beside me so I held her hand, I could tell she was nervous, but she stayed beside me.
The crowd stopped in front of us, and I heard a few of them gasp out loud as they noticed Layla standing beside me, Odin moved forward with tears in his eyes.

"Layla." He said.
Layla let go of my hand and slowly walked towards him, her legs were still wobbly, but she made it without falling.

"Father." She whispered with a croaky voice, and they both hugged, and the crowd cheered.

I smiled, as one by one the crowd moved forward to greet her. I was happy for Odin as I knew he had been waiting for the day he could see Layla in human form again. I glanced back at the gate to the forest and wondered what had happened to Finn, why did he just disappear? Did he have second thoughts about hurting me or did he just assume I would fall and not get help from Layla? As these questions ran through my mind I felt pain on my hand and I noticed why, once I looked down at it, it was dripping blood from a deep gash on my palm where I had grabbed the edge of the cliff. I knew my injuries would heal in a few days thanks to my magic, but it would still need to be cleaned and wrapped up.

Someone took hold of my hand, it was Tristan he looked at my wound with concern and asked,

"What happened?"

"I…. Um…."

Before I could reply, Odin shouted, "Lets go inside, you too Rose."

I glanced at Odin then back at Tristan, he nodded and together we followed the crowd back to the tower.

As we got inside the tower others greeted Layla, but Odin dragged her away to the medical room, I was about to leave and go to my room, but Tristan grabbed my arm and said through our mind link,

"You're not escaping, your injuries need to be checked." And he pulled me to the door.

"Ah…but Tristan." I was trying to come up with an excuse to leave but I could tell Tristan wasn't going to let me, without me getting checked by the doctor first.

"Fine." I said out loud and Tristan smiled and led me through the door.

As we entered the room, I saw Summer taking Layla behind a curtain so she could examine her in private. Doctor Wesley saw me, and I smiled at him and held up my hand. He shook his head and came over to examine the wound.

"Really Rose, you may as well move in, you're in here more than anyone." He said.

"Well blame him, he keeps dragging me in here." I said and pointed at Tristan.

"I wouldn't have to if you kept yourself safe." Said Tristan.

"Even keeping me locked in this tower wouldn't keep me safe." I sighed.

"What do you mean, don't you even trust us now?" Asked Tristan.

"That is not what I meant…" I replied.

"Well, what did you mean?" Shouted Tristan.

"That is enough you two, Doctor can you please see to Rose's injuries. Once she is fixed up, we are going to my office to talk." Said Odin who had heard us.

"Yes of course, come this way Rose I will clean and wrap up your hand and you can tell me about any other injuries you may have." Said Doctor Wesley.

I walked over to another bed and sat down, Stella brought bandages over to us and the doctor got to work cleaning the wound. I could hear Tristan asking Odin how Layla was doing, and I heard Odin reply and tell him she would be alright, but she will need time to adjust to being human again, and I hoped Layla wasn't mad at me for making her change back if she wasn't ready yet.

"So Rose are you hurting anywhere else?" Asked Doctor Wesley as he finished wrapping up my hand.

I hesitated as I wasn't sure if I should tell him about my side hurting, it was where the shadow bear had slammed into me and one of my legs was sore as I had hit the rocks when I fell.

"Rose?" He asked.

"Well, I might have some bruises, but I will be fine, you don't have to check." I replied.

The doctor put his hands on his hips and stared at me, then he shouted, "Odin, can you please come here and explain to Rose that if she tells me about an injury, I always have to check it."

Odin walked over to us and said, "Rose please let the doctor examine you."

"Alright." I said and pulled up my top to reveal a large bruise on my side that had already turned a nasty shade of blue and purple.

"Ouch." Said the doctor and Odin sat down next to me as the doctor examined the bruise.

"It doesn't feel like you have any internal damage and with your ability to heal like a shapeshifter you should be fine tomorrow but if you have any more problems come back and see me, for now though I will go and get you an ice pack." Explained Doctor Wesley and he left.

Tristan walked over to stand near us, and I knew by the look on his face he had also seen the bruise from across the room. I decided not to mention my injured leg as I could feel it getting better already.

"So, was it the Dark Shadow Guild again?" Asked Odin.

I nodded and looked back down at my wrapped-up hand; it could have been a lot worse if Layla hadn't been with me.

Odin put his hand on mine and said, "You're safe now Rose and thank you for bringing Layla back, once Summer is finished with her, we will go to my office and talk. We will protect you, that is our job but also you should know by now you're important to us all."

"I know, thank you, you are all important to me too and really it was Layla who brought me back, she saved me." I said and smiled.

Before Odin could ask any more questions Layla came back from behind the curtain with Summer and she already looked better and was now dressed in the Mystical Knight tracksuit, Odin got up and walked over to them.

The Doctor came back and gave me the icepack then walked over to the others, Tristan sat down next to me, and we both watched them in silence. After a while Layla walked over to us and pointed to my hand and side as she saw the ice pack.

"Oh, I am fine, how are you feeling?" I asked. Layla nodded and pointed at her throat.

Odin walked over and explained, "Layla will be fine she just needs some food and rest, and she needs to get used to being human again, as it has been a while, she can't speak fully yet as it will take time for her mind to catch up with her transformation."

Layla nodded again, put her thumbs up and smiled.

I took the icepack from my side and put it down beside me then I stood up and said, "Thank you for saving me Layla and I'm sorry for getting you into trouble…I…" Before I could finish Layla gave me a hug and I hugged her back.

"Alright I think it is time to talk, lets go back to my office. Tristan, can you gather our team and Dominic." Said Odin and he took hold of Layla's hand and helped walk her to the door.

I started to follow them, but Tristan stopped me and said, "I'm sorry I shouted at you before, I just don't like seeing you hurt."

"It is alright, you are still my best friend." I replied and smiled.

"Good." He laughed and we both followed the others out the door.

While Tristan went to find the others, I followed Odin and Layla to his office.

Chapter 18.
Making Plans.

We had all finally sat down in Odin's office to talk, it had taken a while for everyone to come and when they did arrive they were excited to see Layla. Isabella, Marigold, and Clover had arrived with plates of food and drinks and Layla was now sat next to Odin happily eating. Edmund had also come, and he had brought along Dominic who was also Layla's uncle, he was sat watching her with a big grin on his face.

Also in the room, standing near the door was Tristan's guards Gray and Jaxon, and Councilor Vincent who insisted on being here to make sure he heard the full story and find out what was going on, he was also keeping a close eye on Tristan, and I could tell he was not happy the prince was sat next to me.

"So, who would like to start?" Asked Odin.

"I will. I would like to know why there seems to be more shadow demons appearing lately, does anyone know what their goal is and what are the Mystical Knights doing about it?" Asked Councilor Vincent.

"Well sadly none of us have found anything out yet, we don't know if the main focus is the jewel of darkness or another form of magic or it may even be due to the absence of the king. We are looking into it." Explained Odin.

"I see." Said Councilor Vincent and he wrote something down in his notebook.

"The Kings Guards are patrolling more areas in the city and making sure the kings castle and grounds stay protected." Said Dominic.

"Good, for now we should continue what we have been doing, is that alright Prince Tristan?" Said Odin.

"Yes, that is the best idea, but the king always tells me the main priority is the safety of his people, if the attacks get worse in the city and they are at risk, a lockdown would be the right choice, and we may have to start a curfew to keep them indoors during the night." Replied Tristan.

I smiled, Tristan would truly make a great king one day I bet Lucas was proud and the king had definitely made the right choice.

"Yes, that is a great idea, Prince Tristan." Said Councilor Vincent.

"Very well, we will do that if the attacks happen more in the city. Our main focus should be finding out what the Dark Shadow Guild truly wants and maybe Rose can help us with that." Said Odin and everyone looked at me.

"Me, what can I do?" I asked.
"Well for now you can tell us what happened in the forest." Replied Odin.

"Yes, and don't leave anything out." Said Councilor Vincent.

I glanced at Layla, and she smiled at me and nodded, so I took a deep breath and told them everything about the attack, well except for the part where Finn admitted his boss wanted me to join them, as for some reason I knew I didn't want the Mystic Council to know that yet, but I would tell Odin about it later.

As I finished, the room became silent as everyone took in what I had said, and then Odin spoke,
"Thank you for telling us Rose, I think from now on you should only go to the forest with at least two

guards with you and stay closer to the tower. I'm glad you are both safe."

"Interesting story, tell us, is this the first time you have been attacked?" Asked Councilor Vincent.

I looked down at my hand and wondered if I should tell them about the other time I was attacked.

"Rose? You can tell us." Said Isabella.
I nodded, "There was another time in the forest, but only shadow demons appeared, I hadn't seen Finn since that last time at Greenfield Village. We managed to fight them off without trouble."

"We, who else was with you?" Asked Tristan.
"Layla, I was exploring again, and she managed to come later on to help me." I explained.

"So, my daughter was involved, and you still didn't tell me." Said Odin and he sounded disappointed.

"Why didn't you tell us Rose?" Asked Marigold.
"I'm sorry, I just didn't want to worry you all and you have all been busy with other things. I also wanted to find out myself what was going on and I thought it would be better not to get anyone else involved so no one else would be at risk from getting hurt." I said.

"The fact that you didn't tell us about this is what will put us all at risk, if we did not know about these attacks we would not tighten security and make sure you had someone with you at all times, we would not be able to keep you or the jewel of darkness safe, and Layla was also put at risk trying to help keep you safe alone." Said Dominic.

I didn't know what to say, he had a good point but at the time I didn't think about it like that. So I just nodded and said, "I understand, sorry."

Odin sighed and said, "Well you are both safe, that is what's most important. Just make sure you tell us about everything from now on."

"Alright." I replied, but I felt guilty as I knew I was still hiding something from them, I didn't want them to know I can see Caleb's ghost yet as I would also have to explain about Lucas which I knew would upset them.

"Good, I think the best thing for you now Rose would be to go to your room and rest, you have been through enough today, you don't have to go to your afternoon lessons, but you can study in your room if you wish. And if you do decide to go for another walk please don't go to the forest." Said Odin.

I smiled and nodded; he had noticed how tired I was.

"I will take a team of King's Guards around the area where the attack happened in case any clues were left about their location, and we will do another patrol around the forest." Said Dominic and he got up to leave.

"Yes, that is a good idea, I will go and explain things to the Mystic Council, Prince Tristan you should go back to the castle for now, we will let you know if anything else happens." Said Councilor Vincent.

"Alright." Said Tristan but he did not look happy about it.

"Marigold and Clover please let the Fairy Queen know what happened, I will be taking Layla back home so she can see her family." Said Odin and he smiled at her as she grabbed another sandwich off the plate in front of her and started eating it. I remembered Odin and Layla also had a cottage near the wolf pack in the grounds.

174

Dominic nodded, patted Layla on the head and
walked out the office.

"I will go with Marigold and Clover; it has been a
while since I saw Queen Titania." Said Isabella
and she followed them out the door.

Tristan stood up, nodded at me then he left with
Jaxon and Gray.

"Go and rest Rose, we can talk more tomorrow if
you wish." Said Odin.

"Alright." I said and stood up to leave, I noticed
Layla was waving at me, so I waved back and left
the office.

As I walked back up the stairs Iris stopped me,
she asked, "Are you alright? I heard there was
another attack."

"Yes, I will be fine, how did you hear about it
already?" I asked, as I was shocked the news had
already got around the tower.

"Oh, everyone knows everything around here
and everyone is talking about that wolf girl." She
replied.

"Oh, right." I said.
"Well, I better go, we still have things to do. I will
see you tonight." Said Iris and she started to walk
down the stairs.

"Wait...tonight, what is happening tonight?" I
asked.

She turned back around and looked shocked,
"The student pool party is tonight, didn't you get
the invite?"

"Oh, no I didn't know." I said.
"Liv and Yara were handing out the invites, I'm
sure they just haven't gotten around to giving you
it yet, it is tonight at 6pm in the pool room. Bye."
She said and she hurried off down the stairs

before I could reply.

If Liv was involved in handing out the invites I
wasn't surprised I didn't get one, but I was
surprised it was the first time I had heard about it,
none of the other students had even mentioned it.
Maybe none of them wanted me there, not that I
wanted to go, a pool was not the place I would go
to, to have fun.
I sighed, headed up to my room and closed the
door behind me. I decided to lay down in bed to
rest, I was going to read but my eyes drifted shut
and I fell asleep.

Chapter 19.
Seeing the truth.

I suddenly found myself walking down a dark corridor of an old stone building, I didn't know where I was, I had never been here before, but I did know the girl who was walking beside me, it was Caleb's sister Allena.
Was I somehow seeing her memories?

"Allena." I said, but she didn't answer me, she couldn't hear me I was only here to watch.
  We could hear voices in front of us coming from behind a large door that had gold flowers etched on it, it was open a little, so Allena and I peeped through the gap.
  "You need to find a way to bring the boy to our guild, we need the jewel of darkness for the plan to work." Said a ruff male voice, it didn't sound like a human, was it a monster?
  "I know, but it will be difficult, the boy is a Mystical Knight, and he is close to the shapeshifter king." Said another voice, a woman this time.
  I could see the figure of the woman standing in front of a tall mirror and on top of the mirror was a weird symbol, but I wasn't sure what it meant. No one else was in the room, so where was the other voice coming from? Was it inside the mirror? I thought.
I also realized there was some kind of magic in the room and around the woman, it was stopping me from seeing her face, it was like she was wearing some kind of black veil, and by the way Allena was squinting her eyes, I guessed she couldn't see much either. Though I did know there was a strong

magical aurora coming from inside the room and I
somehow knew the leader of the Dark Shadow
Guild was inside.

"I know you will find a way, after all you were the
one who killed Caleb's parents and blamed it on
the Mystical Knights so he and his sister would
join us and now Caleb is one of our strongest
members. So, think of a plan, we need the jewel of
darkness." Said the creepy monster voice.
   I was shocked but not as shocked as Allena, she
put her hands over her mouth and backed away.

I woke up. I wasn't sure how or why, but I
definitely knew what I saw was a memory and not
just a dream, it had happened, and I realized that
was why Allena wanted to leave the Dark Shadow
Guild, she had learnt the truth, the Dark Shadow
Guild was bad. She didn't just want to leave
though, she wanted to put an end to the lies and
save her brother. So, she asked Lucas for help
and together they had planned to take down the
Dark Shadow Guild from the inside and try to find
proof so Caleb would believe his sister. At first
they had kept it a secret from the Mystical Knights,
only Tristan knew, it was to protect them and
make it more believable but, once Lucas had
become a dark shadow member he realized the
plan had become too risky, so Lucas told the
Mystical Knights about Allena and then persuaded
her to leave the Dark Shadow Guild and go with
him to the Mystical Knights, but someone in the
Dark Shadow Guild had found out they were both
traitors and before they could leave that someone
used dark magic on Allena and it killed her. And
when Lucas saw this, he lost control of the magic

inside the jewel, and he too was lost.

Caleb hadn't believed his sister he always
suspected the Mystical Knights were trying to trick
her and he never trusted Lucas, so when he saw
his sister fall in front of Lucas he assumed it was
the Mystical Knights who had killed her.
I wasn't sure how I knew all this from the
memories and dreams, but I did, and I knew it was
all true.
I had to tell Caleb, he deserves to know the truth
and Allena would want me to at least try and tell
him, but wouldn't he already know, he is a ghost
now, wouldn't he have somehow found out the
truth, but then why would he still want me to join
the Dark Shadow Guild?
I was still confused; a lot of things still didn't make
sense and how was I seeing Allena's memories
and feeling the things she had felt and even
knowing about how Caleb felt about it. I had a lot
of questions, but I knew I was seeing Allena's
memories for a reason, and I knew speaking with
her brother would be the best thing to do right
now, but how do I find him? He only comes to
annoy me when he feels like it.
 "Caleb?" I said out loud.
There was no answer, and he didn't appear, guess
I will just have to wait for him.
I also wondered if this was the right time to tell
Lucas too as he may have more answers, but I
decided to wait longer so I could have more time
to think about it.

I decided to study at my desk and read more
about the Dark Shadow Guild and the jewel of
darkness from the large book Odin had given me.

A lot had happened since finding the book on Odin's desk back at Old House in Greenfield Village. I had learnt a lot, but I knew there was a lot more to learn and my power had grown stronger since then too, the magic in the jewel was becoming more unpredictable and I knew if I didn't find out the truth about the magic stored inside and learn how to control it better it may become too much for me.
I also wanted to find any clues about the strange voice I had heard in Allena's memory and look for the symbol I had seen too.

After a while I slammed the book shut and sighed, I hadn't learnt anything new.
   Suddenly I heard a voice behind me, "I see you're still doing research on us?" Said Caleb.
   I spun around and smiled, "Caleb, you're here."
Caleb looked confused and then he said, "That is the first time you have looked happy to see me."
   "Well, there is something important I have to tell you, I know you won't like what I'm about to say but I think you deserve to know the truth." I said.
   "Go on, I'm listening."
"Um, it is about your sister…" Before I could finish he turned around to leave and said, "Never mind."
   "Wait, I'm seeing her memories." I said.
"What?" Said Caleb and he turned back around.
   "I believe they are her memories; I saw what happened on the day she died and just recently we were walking down a dark corridor, and we stopped outside a large brown door that had gold-colored flowers on it, we heard two voices coming from behind the door. One voice belonged to a woman and the other sounded like a man but also didn't sound human." I said, and then I told him

about their conversation and about how Allena
had tried to team up with Lucas to stop the Dark
Shadow Guild once she had heard they had killed
her parents.

"And that plan ended well didn't it, so did the
Mystical Knights kill her because the plan failed?"
Shouted Caleb.

"No, you don't understand, the Mystical Knights
didn't kill her or your parents. Something dark
killed her, I could feel the magic when I saw the
memory, my guess is someone from your guild
realized Allena and Lucas was planning on leaving
and they were not happy about it." I explained.

"You obviously just felt the jewel of darkness, that
has dark magic too remember. Do you think I
would believe these lies; the Mystical Knights are
messing with your mind too, just like they did with
my sister." He said angrily.

"Look I don't know why I'm seeing these
memories, but I know they are true, why would I
be seeing them if they are lies. It has something to
do with the jewel of darkness I just know it."

Caleb sighed and said, "My sister is dead, I'm
dead. Maybe you are seeing these memories
because of the guilt you feel, what I said before is
still true if you want forgiveness then join my guild.
We can help you better than the Mystical Knights,
you need to learn to control the dark magic soon,
or you will end up like me and my sister." He was
about to fade away again.

"I promise you I will think about joining your guild
if you promise me you will think about what I just
told you and try to find out the truth. Don't do it for
me or even for yourself but do it for your sister." I
said.

He looked at me with sad eyes and then turned around to leave again, but before he faded away he said, "I promise."

I rubbed my eyes, took a deep breath, and wondered if telling him was the right choice, and now that he was a ghost would he even be able to find out the truth or was it already too late. If I did join the Dark Shadow Guild would I be able to find out more about what happened and also find out more about the jewel of darkness and stop the guild from the inside as Allena and Lucas had tried. I shook my head as I knew that was a bad idea and if Lucas and Allena couldn't do that, how was I going to do it?

I suddenly felt a presence outside my door, someone was there. I slowly put my hand on my dagger and got up and walked over to my door, I placed my hand on the door handle and quickly opened the door. The girl standing there jumped back in shock, she was younger than me, she looked the same age as Clover or maybe younger, she had short black hair, and her eyes glowed a bright green. She was a shapeshifter and just by looking at her I could tell she was a big cat, she reminded me of Tristan.

"Hello, do you want me?" I asked her.

"Ah hello, no, I mean yes. Sorry it's just Lucas was my cousin, and I was hoping to get something from his room, but it is probably no longer there, and I didn't want to bother Tristan. I will leave." She said quickly and quietly, and I could tell she was a shy person.

I didn't even know Tristan and Lucas had a cousin, but I could see the family resemblance and I wondered if she could change into a panther too.

"No wait, maybe I can help. What do you need?" I asked and smiled as I spotted Lucas behind her.

"Well, there was a photo of me, Lucas and Tristan standing together, it was on his wall, but I guess it got packed up when you moved in, I should have thought of that." She explained.

I smiled and opened the door, "It should still be here, we wanted to keep up Lucas's memories, please come in." I said.

She hesitated but then walked inside and she smiled as she saw all the photos were still on the wall and the wooden figures of the horses and big cats were on the shelves. She walked over to the wall and looked through the photos.

I joined her and said, "I'm Rose, it's nice to meet you."

She turned to face me and laughed, "Ah, I'm sorry I didn't tell you my name, I'm Maya, it's nice to meet you too. Clover has told me about you, how you all met and how you could see Lucas in mirrors, I wish I had that power." She looked back sadly at the photos.

"So can you see the one you wanted?" I asked her and felt bad I couldn't tell her Lucas was beside her now, smiling at her.

"Yes, here it is." She said and pointed at one of the photos.

I looked at the one she pointed at and saw her when she was younger in a cute blue dress standing between Lucas and Tristan and they were all laughing together surrounded by flowers.

"Tristan's mother took the photo, but she forgot to wait until we were ready, we were laughing too much as Lucas had said something funny. I said we should take another one, but Lucas said he liked this one as it made us look closer, he was silly." Maya explained.

I glanced at Lucas, he looked sad. He noticed me looking at him and he smiled, pointed at the photo then pointed at Maya.

I smiled and said, "You should take it with you, I believe he would want you to have it."

"Are you sure? Maybe Tristan wants to keep them altogether."

"It will be alright; I'm sure Tristan won't mind." I replied and took the photo from the wall and held it out to her.

"Thank you." She said and took it. "I miss him a lot, I wanted to become a Kings Guard so I could help protect him, but I guess I was too late. I will still try to help keep Tristan safe though, and I want to protect the ones Lucas cared for."

Tears welled up in my eyes and I realized I was picking up on Lucas's feelings, but Maya didn't know this, so she said, "Oh no I'm sorry I didn't mean to make you upset."

"No, it is alright, it's not your fault I just felt emotional for some reason, I'm fine." I said quickly and wiped my eyes.

"Oh OK, well I better go now. Thank you for this." Said Maya and she walked back towards the door.

Before she left, I said, "Take care of yourself too, Lucas also cares a lot about you, he would want you to be happy."

Maya glanced back at me with a confused look on her face but then she smiled and nodded then left the room.

I waited to hear she had gone down the stairs before I turned to Lucas and asked, "Are you alright?"

"Yes, well I will be. I didn't know she wanted to become a Kings Guard to protect me. We are cousins but me and Tristan think of her more like a sister, we were close, that is why I didn't say anything aloud as I was afraid she would sense me here and become more upset." Replied Lucas.

I nodded and turned back towards the photos, I bet it was hard for Lucas, he could still see and hear his family and friends, but he could no longer communicate with them, and I bet he still had a lot to say to them too.

I sighed out loud and said, "Sorry."
"Don't apologize Rose, nothing is your fault." He said and he came to stand beside me.

I looked at the gap on the wall where the photo used to be and noticed there was another photo hiding behind the next one so I moved it over so I could see the one beneath it. To my surprise I was on the photo, I was about six-years old wearing a green dress and carrying a basket full of flowers, I was standing in front of the fountain at Greenfield Village and two young boys were standing beside me and I knew straight away they were Lucas and Tristan.

"When. How?" I said and removed the photo from the wall and held it up to Lucas.

"That is me." I said.
Lucas looked at the photo shocked and said, "I remember that day, we had stayed at Old House for the first time and on the last day there was a flower festival in the village, we didn't want to go as we knew the villagers weren't happy about us being there, but our mother wanted to go so we did. I remember you gave us all a flower; no wonder we became friends straight away we had

already met before."

"It is strange though, I don't remember meeting you, I don't remember this day." I said and looked back at the photo.

"Well, you were little, you must have forgotten." He smiled.

"You think I would remember the first time I met a shapeshifter, and I met two."

He laughed, "Four, my parents were there too." "It is weird though, I'm trying to think back to that day, but I can't remember anything at all, I don't even remember being the flower maiden and that was a huge deal in our village."

"Well, a lot has happened to you, sometimes you do forget things from your childhood if a lot crazier things have happened since then." Explained Lucas.

"Yeah, I guess you're right." I said but something didn't feel right about any of this.
I still think I would remember meeting magic users for the first time. My mother told me stories about them, and I always said I would love to meet one, I didn't care if it was a shapeshifter, Fairy or even a human who could use a magical item, I didn't care which one, I just wanted to meet one and make friends. So how is it I have totally forgotten that day, I thought.

"Why don't you go and show Tristan the photo, I bet he would love to find out we all met before." Said Lucas.

"Yeah, I think I will. Though he always seems to be busy. I know he is the prince, so I don't want to cause him more problems." I said.

"Don't be silly Rose, my brother loves seeing you, you're his best friend, you don't cause him any problems. I know if you call him, he will

186

definitely come." Said Lucas and he smiled and pointed at my head.

I smiled; Lucas was right I can use our mind link. **"Tristan, I need to see you, is there any way you can leave the castle and come and visit me?"** I asked.

There was a pause, and I wondered if he had heard me or maybe he couldn't come but then I heard his voice.

"I'm on my way." He replied.

I smiled and told Lucas, "He is coming, but I forgot to tell him where I was, so how does he know?"

"You should know by now Tristan can find you wherever you are, even if your minds were not connected, he still has his panther instincts, remember." Explained Lucas.

"Yeah you are right, how could I forget." I smiled and sat down on the end of my bed, I looked again at the photo in my hand, though maybe I forget more than I thought.

I always thought I was good at remembering the past, I remember a lot from my childhood, I remember nearly everything about my family and friends at Unicorn Stables and all the times we spent together, I remembered how I rescued Silver and helped look after him. I remember the good times and the bad, so why couldn't I remember this day, not one bit of it.

There was a knock at my door, and I knew it was Tristan, I got up and opened the door.

"Hello." We both said at the same time and laughed.

He entered my room and shut the door behind him, "I can't stay long, Gray and Jaxon will realize I'm missing soon. What's up?"

I held out the photo and he took it.

"That is me." I said.

He looked more shocked than Lucas had, "What! I remember this day. It was the last day of our holiday, we stayed at Old House I think it was the first time. Our mother wanted to visit the village; you gave us all a flower even though no one else would come near us. I remember thinking then that all non-magic users weren't bad, you helped me see the good in them." He smiled at me then looked again at the photo.

"I can't believe I forgot about that, I thought you looked familiar when we met but I just assumed I was getting you mixed up with someone else, though your scent was familiar too." Said Tristan.

"Well at least you remember now, it's weird, no matter how hard I try, I can't remember that day at all. I can't remember you or Lucas." I said sadly.

"You can forget things from the past and you were younger; I don't remember all my childhood memories." Said Tristan.

"Yeah, I know, I just thought I would remember meeting shapeshifters for the first time." I said.

I walked over to the desk and picked up a wooden panther figure Lucas had made long ago.
Tristan walked over to the wall of photos and pinned the photo back up.

"Don't worry I'm sure you will start to remember, I'm glad we got to meet as kids, maybe that's why we have a mind link."

"Yeah that could be the reason, maybe I forgot the memory, but my mind somehow knew and connected us because we had met before.... maybe, I think." I said and rubbed my head.

Tristan laughed and said, "Don't give yourself a headache. Whatever the reason, I'm glad we got to meet again and I'm glad you got to really meet Lucas."

Lucas smiled at his brother, and I struggled to hold back the tears.

"Rose?" Tristan had sensed my sadness.
"Ah it's nothing, I'm glad I got to meet you both too." I said and I quickly put the panther figure back down.

"It is a good thing I kept the photos up, otherwise we wouldn't have realized." Said Tristan.

"Actually, we have your cousin Maya to thank, she came to see one of the photos and I told her she could keep it, I hope you don't mind but I found the photo of us beside that one." I explained.

"Really, Maya came here? Well, that's good, it's alright I'm sure Lucas would want her to have it and it helped us." He said.

"That is what I thought, but why didn't you tell me you have a cousin?" I asked.

"Ah sorry, I assumed you already knew, and we haven't had the chance to talk about her. She has been away with her parents, and she only recently moved back here with them, she struggled a lot when Lucas passed away and I wasn't much help to her. She is more like a sister to me and I'm hoping I can be a better brother to her, now that she is back." Explained Tristan.

"It's alright, I understand but don't worry you already are a great brother, Lucas told me... um before." I explained.

"Well, he was better than me but thanks Rose. I better go now before the whole Kings Guards start looking for me...."
Before Tristan could finish we suddenly heard the bells ringing outside.

"Um are those for you." I laughed but I stopped as I noticed Tristan's concern.

"Something has happened, I better go." He said and walked to the door.

"Wait, what do you mean?" I asked.

"When they ring the bells like that, it means they want all the Mystical Knights and Kings Guards to gather outside. You should stay here, and I will...."

I interrupted, "No, I'm coming with you."

And I made sure to grab my sword before I followed him out the door with Lucas beside me.

Tristan sighed but he didn't stop me, and we both ran down the stairs.

Chapter 20.
Danger Approaching.

We got outside and a group of Mystical Knights and Kings Guards were gathered together, I also noticed a few horses had been tacked up and they were waiting nearby with Ethan and Leah. I spotted Odin at the front of the group, Tristan walked over to him, and I noticed Jaxon and Gray moving to the front of the crowd to get closer to him; I managed to get to the front of the crowd too.

"Good, it looks like everyone is here. We have heard reports the Dark Shadow Guild is making its way towards Sunna village and shadow demons have also been spotted. We need to get there now so we can help the villagers and figure out why they are going there. A couple of Kings Guards will be staying here to keep the tower and castle safe while we are gone, and some have already been sent to the city to do patrols and keep the people indoors. The rest of you will be coming with me, we have to move fast to get there in time, mount up." Shouted Odin.

Everyone started to walk towards the horses and the shapeshifters changed into their animal forms, I noticed a few wolves going out the gate first, they must be going on ahead to get there faster. I remember seeing on one of the maps Sunna village is on the outskirts of Sunlight City, so it won't take them too long to get there. I looked at the horses and realized Silver wasn't with them and then I spotted the other students standing near the tower and watching the others leave and I realized they were not going with them.

Odin, Tristan, Jaxon, and Gray started to walk off, so I quickly followed them, Tristan glanced back as he sensed me behind them and then Odin noticed me, he said, "No Rose you are staying here."

"But I can help…" I started to argue but Odin spun around and shouted, "You are not a Mystical Knight yet, you are staying here that is an order."

When he noticed the sad look on my face he sighed and walked over to me, he placed his hand on my shoulder and in a softer voice he said, "I'm sorry Rose but you have to keep the jewel of darkness safe, you have to stay here, it is for the best, we will be back soon." He turned back around and followed the others.

"You better be or I'm coming to get you." I said.

Odin laughed, walked over to the last horse waiting and took the reins from Leah. Tristan nodded at me and then he changed into his panther form and Jaxon and Gray turned into wolves.

I watched as they all left and I had a bad feeling, I hope it didn't turn out like it had last time when I had watched Odin and Tristan leave at Greenfield Village; well, if it did I would definitely be going to save them again.

"**Be careful.**" I said through my mind link and even though I could no longer see him, Tristan answered.

"**Don't worry we will be fine and when we get back, I will take you to see my parents, I think they would like it if they saw you again and it might help you remember.**"

"**Ok, yes I would like that.**" I replied and smiled.
He didn't reply but I knew he had heard me.

Sunlight City, A Mystical Knight Novel book 2.
By Jade Stephenson ©.

"Don't worry Rose they will be alright; they have all trained hard and as the prince my brother has to go, to show his people he cares. Odin is right it is better you stay behind, for now." Explained Lucas, he was still standing beside me.

I sighed out loud and then smiled as Silver appeared beside me, "Have you escaped again." I said and laughed as he nuzzled my hand, I patted him on the neck and Leah walked over to us.

"Ah there you are Silver; I was looking for you. Are you alright Rose?" She asked me.

"Yes, I'm fine, just annoyed I can't go with them to help. I hope Silver hasn't been causing you any trouble." I replied.

"Oh no he is a good boy; he just doesn't like Declan much but I'm sure he will get used to him. I was looking for Silver because all horses that haven't gone with the others on their mission have to be secured in the stables tonight and everyone else has been told to stay indoors to keep safe, I'm just glad we have that pool party tonight to keep us busy." She said.

"Ah right. I will take him back to the stables, I wanted to spend some time with him, and I will make sure he doesn't get out again." I said and laughed as he nuzzled my hair.

"Ok thank you. That will help, I wanted to go see Vivian about my outfit for tonight, bye." Said Leah and she patted Silver on his neck before she hurried off to the tower.

"Come on boy, you heard her. You have to stay in the stables tonight, don't worry I will give you an extra treat." I said and smiled as he followed me to the stables.

I noticed Lucas had gone again and I wondered

where he went when he wasn't with me, was he
back inside the jewel, I thought, and I looked down
at it around my neck and saw it was glowing a light
blue again.

When we got to the stables I noticed all the other
horses that had stayed behind were inside and
they had already been fed and they had
everything they needed for the night. I walked into
one of the empty stables and Silver followed me, I
chose this stable as I noticed Patrick was next
door; Silver spotted him and went to say hello. I
smiled and got to work setting up his bed and I
made sure he had enough food and water, though
I know someone from the yard staff would check
on the horses later and during the night.

After I had done that, I decided to give Silver a
brush, I felt I hadn't spent enough time with him
while I was training to be a Mystical Knight and as
there are others in charge of looking after the
horses all the jobs get done. After working with
horses for so long at Unicorn Stables it had been
hard for me to adjust to just riding Silver when it
was needed and not needing to go muck him out
or feed him, as others would do it, felt weird.
  I finished giving him a brush and went off to the
feeding room to grab an apple for him, when I
went back I noticed Declan sweeping up the yard
and when I stopped outside Silver's stable he
approached me and said, "Your horse needs to be
trained more and you should not be giving him
extra treats, he needs to know we are in charge,
so he listens to orders."
  Silver charged forward to the stable door and
stamped one of his front hooves down on the floor,

194

I had never seen him look so angry at someone
before.

"Silver is perfect the way he is, he is my family,
and he doesn't need training he knows exactly
what to do." I said.

"I see where he gets his rudeness from, I am not
the only one thinking this, he escapes and goes
around as though he owns the place. A horse that
acts and looks like that doesn't belong here, he is
evil, and I know when the king returns he will think
the same." Said Declan.

"Silver belongs here more than you do, what kind
of person working with horses can say all that,
maybe you're the evil one!" I shouted and the
jewel of darkness sparked red, Declan backed
away.

"What is going on in here." Said another voice, it
was a Kings Guard.

"Keep those monsters away from me, she is
cursed. I'm going home." Said Declan and he
walked off.

I took a deep breath, and the jewel faded a little,
"I didn't do anything." I told the Kings Guard.

"Alright but I think you should go back to the
tower now." He said.

I nodded and stroked Silver's nose, "Don't worry
boy, you will be alright just stay away from him." I
whispered and gave him his apple before I left.

As I walked away from the stables I glanced
behind me and noticed the Kings Guard was
watching me, he was probably making sure I was
going back to the tower. I sighed; I couldn't believe
Declan had said those things about Silver, ever
since I met him he has been looking at me with
hatred in his eyes. I assumed it was because I had

the jewel of darkness but maybe there was another reason. I remembered what Caleb had said about Dark Shadow Guild members joining the Mystical Knights and I wondered could Declan be one of them.

I shook my head and decided I would need more proof before telling anyone, just because he hated me and my horse, didn't mean he was working for them, I will ask Ethan and Leah to keep an eye on him.

Once I was back at the tower I quickly grabbed some food from the cafeteria and decided to head to the library to study more, I knew I had to keep my mind busy, so I didn't worry about the others on their mission.

The library was quiet, only Veronica was inside, she said hello, then she continued reading the book she was holding. I left her and went upstairs to the second part of the library to find the books on dark magic and a book on symbols so I could try to find out what the symbol on the top of the mirror in Allena's memory meant.

Once I had collected the right books I decided to sit at the small table I had seen Tristan use before, it was a nice place to sit, and I knew if Lucas or Caleb appeared no one would see me talking to myself. I got to work reading the many books and making notes on the things that may be useful, I studied hard and found clues about the symbol, I think it was somehow related to the dragons, but I wasn't sure fully yet as I couldn't find a matching symbol.

I heard the bell ring on the clock tower in the city, and I realized it was later than I thought, the pool party had already started but I had already

decided I didn't want to go.
I also realized we had not heard from the group
that had gone to Sunna village, I looked out the
small window nearby and noticed it had gotten
dark, which was weird as it normally got dark later
in the summer.

I assumed a storm must be coming but as I
thought this, something didn't feel right and then
the lights suddenly went out, the tower went dark.

Chapter 21.
Tower in the Dark.

My eyes adjusted to the darkness and the jewel of darkness lit up to help light my way, but something didn't feel right, and the jewel wasn't as bright as it had been in the past.

"Rose, are you still here?" Shouted Veronica.
"Yes, I'm over here." I shouted and headed in her direction.

She came from behind one of the bookshelves carrying a lamp with a small flame to help guide her.

"Are you alright?" I asked her.
"Yes, I'm fine, luckily I had this lamp already lit on my desk." She replied.

"Yes, luckily I have this." I said and pointed at the jewel of darkness, though it was starting to fade a little more.

"Oh, your magic still works, the light stones have all gone out, I wonder what is wrong." Said Veronica.

Before I could reply we suddenly heard screaming.
"What…." Started Veronica but stopped as we heard more shouting.

"Come on, we better go and see what is happening and check the others are alright." I said, Veronica nodded and followed me to the door.
We left the library and I quickly pulled out my sword from its sheath, I sensed danger.
The whole tower was in darkness, and it wasn't just the lights being off, it felt dark too as though some dark magic was around the tower. The

shouting was coming from the first floor, I looked at Veronica she nodded again, and we headed down the stairs.

As we got down the stairs a shadow demon appeared and ran towards us, Veronica screamed and jumped back and the flame flickered in the lamp but luckily it stayed lit, I used my sword to defeat it. A Kings Guard was also fighting off a demon and I also spotted two Kings Guards near the door holding flame torches, we headed towards the door, and I heard one of the men say,

"How the hell did shadow demons get inside the tower without us seeing them." I noticed it was Hector.

"I don't know but they are all over the tower, the top floors are full of them, we were lucky nearly everyone who stayed behind was in the pool room. We need to make sure everyone is outside and call for back up." Said Aaron who had followed us to the door, once he had defeated the shadow demon.

"This is definitely a bad time for the Mystical Knights to be away." Said Veronica.

"Ah good you are both safe, you two were the last ones inside, we were about to go back upstairs to get you, the Dark Shadow Guild is attacking us, and the tower is swarming with demons, we are all heading outside to the bell towers to call for help." Explained Hector as we all walked outside.

I heard Veronica gasp beside me, all around the tower was a huge black globe and a few King's Guards were banging their swords against it to try and break it so we could all get out.

"You! Take that thing down now, we need to get

out." Shouted Liv as she spotted me.

"Yes, Rose we don't need protecting in here, we need to leave." Said Councillor Vincent.

"I .....I didn't put that up; it is not my magic." I tried to explain.

"Ha! Please, don't make me laugh, that is exactly like the one you put up before." Yelled Liv and I noticed a few others nod in agreement.

"No, I swear it wasn't me." I shouted.
Before anyone else could argue more, Veronica said, "She is right, this isn't Rose's magic. See the runes around the barrier, this is a dark circle from the Dark Shadow Guild, and you can only put it up from the outside." She pointed to the strange symbols on the ground outside the barrier and my heart skipped a beat as I recognized a few from the time Odin, Tristan and the others were trapped in a similar one at Greenfield Village.

"Yes, I see it too. Is there any way to break the barrier? Some of these wounds need more treatment and I only managed to grab my small bag of medical supplies before we had to leave." Said Doctor Wesley who was sat with Yara while Stella wrapped her arm up in a bandage.

I noticed a few others had injuries, Joseph had a leg wound and Summer was helping him.
And a Kings Guard was sat near us, and he held a cloth up against a nasty wound on his head.

The others must have got hit hard while they were at the pool party and patrolling the rest of the tower and I wondered why the shadow demons hadn't attacked me and Veronica in the library.

After Veronica looked more closely at the symbols she answered, "No sadly this particular barrier can only be broken from the outside too and only by someone who can understand the symbols and use some fairy magic, and sadly the ones who could do it either left on the mission or is in the fairy realm at a gathering."

She glanced at Iris, Ebony, Terran and Summer, the four fairies in the barrier and they nodded in agreement.

"Maybe I could try." I said.

"No Rose if you use magic inside a dark barrier it will drain your energy, isn't that right Veronica?" Said Vivian.

"Yes that is right, it can be dangerous if you use too much magic, even the shapeshifters are struggling." Replied Veronica.

Before I could reply, a large black bear suddenly ran out of the tower roaring.

"Ryan, are you alright?" Shouted Hector.

Ryan was followed by two more Kings Guards and one of them shouted, "The blockage is down, get ready, the other shadows have pushed through to the first floor, they are coming out!"

Another Kings Guard left the tower, and he was dragging his injured friend behind him, Doctor Wesley quickly ran forward to help him.

We all backed up against the barrier, careful not to touch it just in case it could hurt us and then we drew our weapons ready to fight.

"Stand together, we can beat them." Shouted George as he stood beside Ethan and Leah.

T.J. changed into his bear form and Jasper stood beside him already a wolf, there were other Kings Guards who also changed into their wolf forms, even though their energy would fade faster they knew fighting in their animal forms would be better for them, to defeat as many shadow demons as they can.

The shadow demons pushed out of the tower doors and charged at us, they were in many forms but mainly in a human or wolf form, trying to hurt us with weapons or bite us. You could hear the clang of everyone's weapons as we fought the demons back, the other students, Leah, Ethan, Matthew, and Alice were still in their swimming gear but luckily they had gotten hold of some weapons, probably from the storage room in the basement.

Two wolves pounced onto the shadows before they could get closer to us, after taking out another demon I looked at the doors of the tower and noticed more were coming, their red eyes glowed angrily as they moved closer, it did not look good for us. We needed to get out of the barrier, I noticed a Kings Guard near the barrier trying to call for help using an S.C.D.,

"Come in! Can anyone hear me, the tower is under attack, I repeat we are under attack, we need back up!" He shouted.

I could tell by the look on his face it was not working, I also noticed the shapeshifters were getting more tired as they fought back the shadow demons as the dark barrier sucked up their energy and magic. The dark barrier needed to come down so I ran up to it and placed my hand on it and sent my magic through it to try and bring it down, but it wouldn't work, and I could feel my energy fading.

"Rose stop! It is no use, that won't work and you're losing your strength." Shouted Matthew as he ran up beside me.

I stopped and looked at him and Alba beside me as I tried to get my breath back, he was right, and I needed my strength to fight.

I smiled and said, "Yeah you're right but I had to at least try something."

"Yeah, poor Alba tried too, he tried to dig out, but some kind of magic zapped his paws." Explained Matthew and he looked at Alba sadly and patted him on the head.

"Stop that, don't fuss I'm fine, but he is right we can't get out that way, we need to think of something else." Said Alba, and Snow hopped over to his side.

I nodded and looked outside the barrier then I opened my mind link with Tristan.

"Tristan if you can hear me, the tower is under attack. Please come back we need help." I said.

I knew he wouldn't hear me, he was too far, and the dark barrier was probably blocking it too, but it was also worth a try.

I was about to get back to the fight to help the others, but I suddenly noticed someone outside the barrier, and I smiled as I realized who it was, it was Layla back in her wolf form.

"Layla! We are stuck in here; can you find the Mystical Knights and bring them back home?" I shouted.

She ran up to the barrier and snarled.

"Rose, look out!" Yelled Vivian behind me and I stepped to the side just in time to avoid an attack from a wolf shadow demon.

I used my sword to defeat it and turned back around to Layla and shouted, "Don't worry we can handle this, just go and find help."

One of the Kings Guards in wolf form ran forward and howled at her, Layla howled back and then she took off at a fast run towards the gate that led to the city, and I hoped she understood what we needed.

I took a deep breath and turned back to help the others fight, we fought with all our strength and tried our best to push the demons back and defeat them but more kept coming out of the tower and I wondered how they all got in there and where were they coming from, was there a dark portal inside and was Caleb or Finn responsible?

"It is no use; more are coming out; at this rate we won't make it." Shouted Liv.

"Don't give up, help will come soon." Shouted Doctor Wesley who was also now fighting to protect the injured, but I also heard him say, "I hope."

We heard a loud bang inside the tower and then the windows on the first floor smashed as more demons jumped out.

"Damn, get ready!" Shouted Hector.

As the others stood ready to fight more, I decided I would do whatever it took to protect them, so I put my sword back in its sheath and ran forward to get in front of them, then I quickly knelt down and put my hand to the ground. My magic shield grew up and wrapped around me and the others to protect them, I knew using the spell of protection will be difficult, but I knew it was also the only way everyone could get some rest and stay safe until help could arrive.

"Rose, are you crazy, you shouldn't be using your magic in here, it's too risky." Shouted Veronica.

"I'm fine." I lied.

The shadows slammed against my shield and hissed at me; I could already feel my energy was fading. I also noticed the shadow demons were not disappearing when they touched my shield as they usually would, I was giving it all I had to hold my shield up, but I knew I couldn't stop as I knew the others needed to rest.

"Rose don't push yourself too hard, if you need to stop, we can still fight." Said Doctor Wesley.

"Yes Rose, don't try to be a hero and get yourself killed, no one would want that." Said Iris.

"Don't worry about me, just try to get some rest and bandage your wounds, my magic might fail so keep your guard up and let me know when the Mystical Knights get here." I replied.

"Thank you Rose, but the others are right, please be careful." Said Leah.

I nodded but I couldn't say anything more as I needed to concentrate, another shadow demon crashed against my shield and hissed, and I gasped and placed both my hands up against my shield and I somehow managed to push more magic into it to strengthen it further.

I knew I wouldn't last much longer hopefully the others will be back soon with Layla.

I suddenly heard a howl in the distance and smiled. I also felt Tristan's mind link through the dark barrier, but we still couldn't talk. I then heard horses running fast on the road from the city, help had finally come.

As the Mystical Knights got closer we could hear them yelling as they realized we were trapped behind a dark barrier.

"The Mystical Knights are back Rose, and it looks like they are trying to break us out the barrier." Said Matthew beside me.

"I will go and see if I can help translate the runes." Said Veronica.

I gasped as my magic shield flickered, and a few shadow demons broke through. Matthew, Jasper, T.J., Ryan, and Hector managed to destroy them before they could get to me or the others. Having two bears in here was definitely a big help, they both stood beside me to guard me from any other attacks.

"Sorry…." I gasped and strengthened my shield again, but I was starting to feel dizzy.

"It is fine Rose; we are ready to fight if you need to drop your shield." Said Doctor Wesley and he placed his hand on my shoulder.

I nodded and said, "Tell me when the dark barrier is down, then I will drop my shield."

"Right." Said Matthew, and we heard more shouting behind us.

"Damn it Rose, you shouldn't be using your magic in there it could kill you!" Shouted Odin.

I slowly took one hand from the shield and put my thumb up in the air to let him know I was fine, even though I knew I wasn't, I knew if he could see my face, he would be even angrier with me. I noticed the doctor leave my side and I heard him walk over to the others, he must have explained my plan as Odin shouted, "Ok Rose, Isabella and Marigold are going to take the barrier down, stay with us."

"Rose, we are nearly done, everyone get ready. The dark barrier will be down in 3,2,1, Now!" Shouted Isabella.

I screamed and used the last of my energy to take down my shield and send my magic towards the shadow demons to destroy as many as I could, before I collapsed to the ground. As my eyes drifted shut, a panther and a wolf stood on guard beside me.

Chapter 22.
One week later.

Today I decided it was time to get out of bed and go outside to see Silver, as Clover had said he had been hanging around the tower waiting for me. My injuries had healed, and my energy had come back but I knew I still wasn't a hundred percent, and my magic still felt weak, I knew seeing Silver would cheer me up.

I looked around the medical room, after the attack on the tower I had passed out and woken up three days later with a grumpy panther sitting beside me. The Mystical Knights were not happy I had been hurt again and they were annoyed the Dark Shadow Guild had led them away on a fake mission so they could attack the tower. The shapeshifters who live in the cottages were also attacked but luckily everyone was now safe; they had wanted to help us but couldn't get to us, only Layla had managed to come and help.

A few of the students had minor injuries and some of the Kings Guards had also been hurt but as most were shapeshifters they had healed earlier and were already back to work and helping the others repair the tower and grounds.

I was alone now in the room, but I could hear many voices outside, everyone was doing their best to help get the place back to normal, and as they had heard the shapeshifter king would be returning soon from his trip away to the mountains, they wanted it perfect for his return, luckily the king's castle didn't get too damaged.

After I had a shower, I felt a lot better, so I headed

off outside, but I didn't get very far, as Summer
had spotted me at the door.

"And where are you going? You still haven't fully
recovered yet." She said.

"I'm just going outside to get some fresh air; I feel
a lot better now." I replied and smiled, Summer
and Doctor Wesley had been having a hard time
keeping me in bed, I wasn't a very good patient.

"Alright fine but don't go too far and no riding
Silver, you're not ready for that yet." She said.

"You need to stop worrying I'm fine really. I'm just
going to go see Silver, I won't ride him, and I
promise I will stay out of trouble." I said and I
quickly walked out the door before she could stop
me.

"You better." I heard her shout behind me as I left.

I smiled again but it soon faded as I left the tower
and saw all the damage caused by the shadow
demons, the others had been in a tough fight after
I had passed out. The fences were broken, some
walls had come down, plants had been damaged
and the ground still had patches of blackness were
it had been burnt by dark magic. I couldn't see
Silver around the tower, so I carried on walking
towards the stables, I passed some Kings Guards
fixing one of the fences, they didn't look happy to
see me, only Ryan who was with them back in his
human form waved at me. I waved back and
carried on walking, I also saw Terran using his
fairy magic to help some flowers grow, as I passed
him, he smiled and winked at me, and I smiled
back. At least everyone didn't believe the rumors
about me being the cause of the shadows
attacking.

I finally got to the stables, more out of breath than

I normally would be, and I smiled as I spotted Silver, he saw me and trotted over to greet me.

"Hello Silver, I'm alright. How are you feeling?" I asked him.

He neighed and I knew he was alright, luckily the stables hadn't been attacked so the horses had stayed safe. As I stroked his neck, I noticed Ethan walking towards us.

"Hello Rose, are you feeling better now?" He asked me.

"Hello Ethan, yes, I'm ok now. How are you and Leah doing?" I asked.

"Our injuries weren't too bad, just a few scratches and bruises, so we are alright now. Things would have been a lot worse if you hadn't been there to put up your shield, so thank you." He replied.

"I'm glad you are both alright and thank you for taking care of Silver for me while I was resting." I said and Silver nuzzled my head.

"I didn't do too much, he was out in the forest or standing near the tower waiting for you most of the time, I think he was worried about you." Said Ethan and we both laughed as Silver nuzzled Ethan's head too.

I was glad Silver was alright and happy, he had settled into his new home quicker than me, even though he was out exploring the forest most of the time, I didn't mind as he was free to live his life the best he could, and I wasn't going to stop him.

We suddenly heard a commotion coming from the horse arena, I looked over and saw Declan shouting at a tall grey horse. He was trying to get him to run but even from where I was stood I could tell he didn't want to, and the horse looked stressed.

"That is Desi our new horse, Declan said he needed more training before anyone should ride him, but Desi let Leah ride him just fine before without problems, so I don't know what's wrong." Ethan explained and he looked annoyed.

Silver sensed Desi was stressed so he started to walk off towards them.

"Easy Silver, you wait here, I will go and help." I said, as I knew if Silver got involved Declan would be in trouble, and so would I as I knew Declan still hated us.

I climbed over the fence and headed towards Declan and Desi. Declan was so angry he didn't even notice me, but Desi did, he saw me, and he neighed and trotted over to my side.

"You stupid horse, I said canter not trot." Declan shouted and he raised the whip in his hand and was about to whip him, but he stopped as he realized I was stood there.

"What is wrong, do you need help?" I asked him.

"Get out of here, I don't need help from you. I'm training this horse, go and train your own." He yelled.

"Well, I can tell Desi doesn't want to be trained by you, he doesn't like to be whipped, and he certainly doesn't like to be called names. You should leave." I said and I moved in front of Desi to protect him.

"I'm warning you Rose, stay out of my way. You don't belong here; you should accept the Shadow Guild's offer and go be with them." He said.

"What do you mean?" I asked, and I suddenly realized only members of the Dark Shadow Guild would know about them asking me to join them.

"Oh please, you know what I mean. You have darkness in your heart, I can tell." He replied and smiled.

"You're the one who is threatening me and the horses, tell me, when did you join the Dark Shadow Guild, was It before or after you got the job here?" I asked and I could tell by the look on his face I was right, he was a member of the Dark Shadow Guild.

"You stupid girl, are you trying to hide your own darkness by lying now. No one will believe you." He said and I realized he was still trying to hide the fact he was one of them.

I tried to stay calm and said, "The moment I met you, and when I saw how bad Silver acted near you, I knew something was off, but I thought I was jumping to conclusions because I knew you hated me. At first, I assumed it was because I held the jewel of darkness, I thought you believed it is a curse, like so many others but that is not it at all, you want the jewel of darkness for yourself and your guild, and you hate the fact that I have it and you can't reach it. And I bet you were involved somehow with the dark barrier because you were the only one who had not gone on the mission with the others and didn't get trapped inside it when it happened."

Declan smirked, "So I guess you aren't as stupid as I thought, but do you really believe the Mystical Knights can help you with that, it will be better with me." He said and he pointed at the jewel.

"You're not getting this jewel, and when I tell the others who you really work for, I bet you won't have a job here anymore." I said and backed away.

"Please, you think they will believe you. You're the one who holds the cursed jewel. You have no proof and I suggest you keep your mouth shut, stay out of my way, and leave now." Said Declan.

"Tell me, what is the Dark Shadow Guild's plan? And I am not leaving you with the horses." I said and I stood my ground.

"I'm not telling you anything. It is time I punished you too!" He shouted and he raised the whip to strike me.

Fear and anger welled up inside me and as I raised my arm to block his attack, I remembered the pain of being whipped before, when I was a little girl trying to save Silver. The jewel of darkness reacted to my feelings and my magic power sizzled up all around me and then it shot towards Declan, before the whip could touch me. The magic hit him, and he flew through the air and landed in a heap on the ground. He wasn't the only one, a few others that were around the stables got knocked to the ground with the force of my magic, and fences also got smashed, the horses neighed and stamped their hooves, but luckily them and the stables were fine.
I took a deep breath to try and calm down and the jewel dulled down a little, but it was still glowing a shade of blue and red and somehow it felt as though my magic had restored to full power again. I realized Declan hadn't moved on the floor, so I started to walk over to him to see if he needed help.

"Declan…. Are you alright?" I asked.
Before I could get closer to him a dagger surrounded by magic suddenly flew through the air and stabbed Declan who was still on the ground. I heard someone scream; it was Liv.

She jumped up off the floor and ran to Declan. "Declan, are you alright?" She asked him.

I noticed a few others getting up off the floor and two Kings Guards ran over to also check on Declan.

"Rose, what have you done?" Asked George who had also ran over.

"I...." I didn't know what to say; that wasn't my magic. Was it? but even I wasn't sure. No, it can't have been the jewel of darkness. Had I killed someone else? I thought.

Luckily, I heard one of the Kings Guards say, "He is still alive, but he needs treatment, we need the doctor."
Desi and Silver came to stand beside me, and Silver nuzzled my head, I knew I had made the right decision to defend the horses, even though the jewel had took it too far, I knew it had only reacted to protect me and the horses. And deep down I knew it wasn't my magic that had caused the dagger to hurt Declan, it hadn't felt right, I looked around at the crowd, but I couldn't see anyone who looked suspicious.
I suddenly noticed Tristan and more Kings Guards running towards us, Tristan glanced at Declan on the floor and then he noticed me, he walked towards me and asked, "Rose, are you alright, what happened?"
Before I could reply, Councilor Vincent shouted, "You should be asking us that question Prince Tristan. We are not alright."

And I noticed two guards were helping him off the floor and I sighed as I realized he had been near the stables too, when it had happened.

"I can tell you what happened, she attacked Declan when he was trying to train that horse and the rest of us got caught in the blast. You should be asking if he's alright, look at him, she stabbed him with a dagger." Shouted Liv and she pointed at Declan who was still unconscious on the floor.

"That is not…." I started to explain but I heard others agreeing with Liv.

Councilor Vincent had gone to check on Declan, I saw a Kings Guard whisper something in his ear, then Councilor Vincent walked over to Tristan and said, "Remember Prince Tristan it is against the law to use magic to attack someone."

Tristan looked back at Declan on the floor and looked at the others stood around him then he looked back at me, and my heart dropped as he said,

"Rose Ashley, I am placing you under arrest for using magic on another. Guards take her away."

THE END, TO BE CONTINUED.

MYSTICAL KNIGHT

Sunlight City, A Mystical Knight Novel book 2.
By Jade Stephenson ©.

Author's notes.

'After writing book 1 The Magical Jewel I knew I
wanted to write another two books, so I got to
work straight away. The ideas came to me easier
this time and book 2 got done faster and I am also
working on book 3.
More characters have been added in these books
and it was fun to think of how to add them to the
book and come up with their stories in my head, all
of my characters have back stories but not all of
them are told in the books, I have also drawn all
the characters to help me understand how to
describe them and so I know who they are and
why they are in the story.
Moving the main character Rose to a new location
was also something I wanted to do, I knew I
wanted her to try and become a Mystical Knight in
the future so moving her to Sunlight City was
always where I wanted her to go, and I also
wanted all the main characters to grow in the
future books to make the story better.
I also knew I wanted to add more emotion to the
books, as I know from reading other books, that's
what makes the story stand out, as I write it helps
to imagine what it would look like on screen, as
though I was watching a movie or a TV series, so I
can understand where the story is going and how
each character is linked and what part they will
play in the story.'

I would like to thank Amazon for making it possible
for me to self-publish my books. I would also like
to thank everyone who bought and read my first
book and gave me good feedback and advice for
book 2, I really appreciate it.

Sunlight City, A Mystical Knight Novel book 2.
By Jade Stephenson ©.

I would like to dedicate this book to my wonderful family and friends who help me through life, and to all the animals of the world.
To the readers who have also bought my second book and continue to support me, writers like me need all the help you can give, to get our stories to more readers so thank you.

About the Author.

Jade Stephenson.

Grew up around North Yorkshire and Teesside, she loves to go on walks with her family and enjoys spending time with her rabbit Thumper, who she has also written stories about too. This is her second novel, and she hopes to write more in the future.

Books By This Author.

The Magical Jewel, A Mystical Knight Novel Book 1.

'It could have happened to anyone but instead it happened to Rose Ashley, her dog found a jewel and her life changed forever, and it will never be the same again. Surrounded by magic, mayhem, fairies and a shapeshifter she will have to make some difficult choices and learn how to control the magic inside. The Mystical Knights come to her aid, but can she trust them?'

Sunlight City, A Mystical Knight Novel Book 2.

'Rose Ashley has arrived at Sunlight City to start her training to become an official Mystical Knight but as the Jewel of Darkness becomes stronger and harder for her to control, she soon learns her training isn't going to be so easy. The Dark Shadow Guild returns, and danger awaits her around every turn. Can she trust everyone around her or is it already too late?'

Sunlight City, A Mystical Knight Novel book 2.
By Jade Stephenson ©.

<u>Rabbit Tails, Christmas Special. The Adventures of Flower and Thumper.</u>

'It is Christmas and the rabbits, Flower and Thumper wake up to have a day of fun with their family. Also you can color in pictures and complete puzzles to help Flower and Thumper have more fun at Christmas.'

Printed in Dunstable, United Kingdom

63262662R00127